D0771545

other
WOMEN

Evelyn Lau

other WOMEN

Vintage Books
A Division of Random House of Canada

Canadian Cataloguing in Publication Data
Lau, Evelyn
    Other women
ISBN 0-394-22497-3
I. Title
PS8573.A78074 1996   C813'.54   C95-931849-6
PR9199.3.L38074 1996

Printed and bound in United States of America
10 9 8 7 6 5 4 3 2 1

I would like to thank the Canada Council for its generous award of a "B" grant; Doug Pepper and Sarah Davies at Random House for their enthusiasm and understanding; Crawford Kilian for looking at yet another early draft; and Tera Coughlin for her home in Los Angeles.

I would especially like to thank my agent, Denise Bukowski, for discerning the final structure of the manuscript.

Several chapters of *Other Women* first appeared, in somewhat different form, in *Canadian Fiction Magazine, Canadian Forum, The Capilano Review, Paragraph, Prairie Fire* and *Quarry*.

For John Updike, whose own books provided me with a constant source of solace during my writing of this one.

...In discontented peace,

in boredom and tolerance, only adultery proves

devotion by risk; only the pulse of betrayal

makes blood pelt in the chest as if with joy.

—Donald Hall,

from *The One Day: A Poem In Three Parts*

The belief that a person has a share in an unknown life

to which his or her love may win us admission is, of all the

prerequisites of love, the one which it values most highly

and which makes it set little store by all the rest.

—Marcel Proust,

from *In Search of Lost Time (Swann's Way)*

1.

Raymond comes to the door dressed in black, wearing the face of the man she loves. His skin is the texture of stone, his eyes narrow and changeable; it is the face of someone for whom making a living means causing hurt to others.

It is not the face of someone in pain. That is the one Fiona wears when she walks towards his hotel room, and sees herself in the mirror at the end of the hallway, her body emerging inside the antique frame knotted with vines and roses. Her dark hair is loose around her shoulders, and her eyes are the colour of amber from the Baltic Sea. Her hands are an artist's hands, the fingers long and pale; her mouth is soft, red, always ready to apologize. Men regard it as her best feature.

She stands before his door, knocking. If he were on the other side, holding his breath, gazing through the peephole, he would see her face distorted as if in grief or sexual desire. She leans her forehead against the cool white wood, thinking she hears movement inside the room, his whispering voice, a rustle of fabric, a telephone cord dragged across a mahogany desk. She knows he is talking to his wife. She knocks for a while longer—stealthily, like a lover, and then sharply and impatiently, like a maid making her morning rounds.

It is then that he comes to the door, opens it, steps back and looks at her with the direct, disinterested gaze of a stranger. It is a look someone passing her on the street might give, indifference edged with a sharp dislike.

"We have to talk," Raymond says.

She sees it is about to happen again.

Two of the walls in his room on the thirtieth floor are made of glass and look out upon the city. At this height his windows are parallel with the windows of the financial institutions across the street, their offices and boardrooms empty until the morning. Raymond sits on one end of the sofa by the window across from the bed, waiting for her to join him. Beside his elbow, on the end table, a rose droops in a bud vase. If she were to hold it in the palm of her hand it would feel silky as a sparrow's breast; it would feel like his warm scrotum when he guides her hand between his legs and says, hoarsely, Hold me there.

"You know what I'm about to say, don't you," he says now, acknowledging that she remembers the other times, the other scenes.

She sits beside him and he turns away from the window to face her. Quickly, he reaches out and touches her wrist, below a corner of her sleeve. It is as wounding as if he had sliced her there with a blade; the shock of it vibrates along her arm. There is nothing tender about the touch, the flick of his fingers. He looks at her like a man in a hurry might look at a traffic light, waiting for it to change; he looks at her like a shopper looks at the person ahead of him at the cash line, the one who pulls out a cheque-book to pay for one or two small items.

"Fiona," he says, "you know how important my marriage is to me. You know I love my wife."

3

Fiona sees his white face through a blur, as if through tears, but she can still see the hard line of his mouth, and that he is not blinking.

"When I look at my wife," he continues, "I see the face of the woman I want to be looking at when I am old."

His face in bed the night before rises in her mind—the backdrop of the city she lives in outside the windows, the cream-coloured sheets around their bodies, the three lines she counted beneath his eyes. She had seen with the shock of revelation the face of the man *she* wanted to be looking at when she opened her eyes some morning twenty or thirty or forty years from that night. It was a face that already bore the signs of age; in the light from the table lamp she noticed the pouches in his skin that would grow heavier and darken with the years, the miniature fans of wrinkles at the corners of his eyes. It was the face she sometimes saw in her dreams, the dreams that woke her in the middle of the night when she was alone.

Fiona had told Raymond what she felt for him. He had buried his face in the pillow; she'd looked at the line of his back, his warm, curved shoulders and his soft hair lit by the yellow lamplight, and the love she felt rose in such a physical wave she had to swallow to keep it down. Then he was holding her arms and shaking her and saying, "You know I love my wife. You know as soon as I saw her I knew she was the person I wanted to be with. In fifteen years that hasn't changed"... and his eyes were wet, and when she held him against her, she felt his tears on her breasts. If she had looked, then, in the mirror across the room she would have seen her suffering face and would not have recognized it as any of the faces she had worn before in front of a mirror. It was a face she might have laughed at on someone else.

"Nothing good can come of this," he says now. "I can't give myself to you, I can't be your lover."

Yet there were the nights that had shaped the past fifteen months of their lives, nights that convinced her she was alive. When they kissed and bit each other until their lips and nipples were bruised and marked, when she drew the length of his penis into her mouth, when his fingers dented her thighs. Although she had never felt him inside her, although he had never released a flood of semen into her, in her mind what they did together had been enough to make her think of him as her lover. Already she had become absorbed into his body, as if into quicksand.

"You know how I feel about you," she says now.

"It will pass," he says. "Give it time."

When the telephone rings he is up from the couch as quickly as an animal leaping from an opened cage. It is Helen, his wife. Fiona knows this even before he picks up the receiver, before his shoulders tighten and he begins to pace, two steps to one side and then two steps to the other, leashed by the curling cord. She hears the tonal change in his voice, how it softens; it is a voice grown intimate, familiar, and it is a voice he has never used with her. She watches him pace beside the bed, its covers now smooth as the layer of icing on a fresh cake.

"Hi, how are you?" he says. "Yes… yes… no. No. I do, Helen. Yes. Tomorrow. Yes… no, first thing. Mmm… I don't know. No. No."

Fiona closes her eyes. Please, she thinks, please, just turn around and look at me. Just that, nothing else. Just turn around and look at me when you talk to her, let me know I am a part of what is happening here.

He does not look at the woman on the couch. He is standing in the path of the lamplight by the bed, the lamplight that had fallen on their faces and bodies the night before, that had covered them like pollen. He does not glance at her, does not even shift his shoulders towards her. If he were not speaking mono-syllabically, one would think he was alone in the room with the voice of his wife. Fiona realizes that with his hunched shoulders, his body turned away from her, he is protecting his wife from her—like a parent shielding a child from the cold or the dark, or from the jealous eyes of barren strangers.

"What?... No. No. Nothing's wrong."

Fiona realizes his wife must be asking why he is talking to her like this. If Helen were in the room, she would understand; she would see the shape of her husband's body, curved around the phone, curved around her voice, keeping it safe from the woman who sits a short distance away on the sofa by the window, perfectly still, who does not make a sound. But who *could* make a sound, who could scream his name, his wife's name, who could scream past his protective body and across the distances, her own name. Fiona!

7

She wonders how much she could get out before he reacted. If she could say, I love your husband. If she could say, Helen, Helen, I love him. What could he do then?

"No, nothing's wrong... Yes. Cross my heart."

Although she does not move from the couch, Fiona feels herself stagger. She thinks that all he has to do is turn a few degrees, look at her, acknowledge her presence, and then she would be all right. Yet if he does not, she could still open her mouth now as easily as she had opened her mouth to take in his penis when he parted his thighs; she could open her mouth and, with just a few words, enter Helen's life.

"Yes, yes. I will. I love you too," he says to the woman on the other end of the phone. "I'm coming home tomorrow."

Fiona has drifted slightly outside her body, and now she looks at herself sitting on the sofa in the softly lit room. A half-full bottle of mineral water is standing on the glass table in front of her, and she has a sudden urge to find the cap that would fit over its neck, screw it on and put the bottle back inside the minibar. But the cap is nowhere nearby; probably he

has thrown it away. She sees the petals of the droop-
ing rose flutter slightly above its reflection in the polished wood of the end table: barely perceptible, but it
is motion. The lamplight in the room is the same
warm gold as the lamplight in her parents' house, in
the impoverished neighbourhood where she grew up.
This gives the hotel room a feeling of familiarity that
she realizes he does not share. After all, his own mem-
ories of lamplight would be different.

"I love you too," she hears him say again, not sure
whether he actually says this or if it is an echo of what
he had said a moment before. Raymond is leaning
against the bedside table, running his free hand
through his hair. Fiona watches him talking, his
mouth close to the receiver. If he is afraid, he does not
show his fear. His voice does not tremble or shake. He
is a good liar, but she suspected that about him when
they first met at the out-of-town arts awards ceremony where he spoke, his delivery smooth and
charming as a sociopath's. It made no difference; two
weeks later when he came to her city, his hard, chilly
face softened between her hands, and his mouth
parted upon hers. Now she watches him pick up a

hotel pen from the pad tucked under the base of the lamp, click it three times, lay it back down on the table. He resumes pacing. In her mind she hears him say, I love you too, I love you too. He had deliberately given his voice feeling when he said it. She thinks that they are probably the sort of married couple who vow they will always mean it when they say they love each other, that they'll never sound as if they're ordering from room service or calling the concierge when they say those words.

Eventually he puts down the phone and walks back to the sofa. Fiona clears her throat as if she is about to give a speech; she straightens her back, pulls the edge of her skirt over her knees, refolds her hands. He sits down and looks at her, waits for her to speak, his face empty of expression.

The night before he had held her naked body and stroked her hair and said, "You will end up hurting me. Please, when you do it, just make it quick. And leave Helen out of it."

"Oh God," she had said, "I don't want to do any-thing to hurt you."

Their skin was bronzed in the lamplight of her

childhood; she leaned her breasts into his face and he bit her nipples and streaked her skin with his tears.

Everything is changed now. This time he does mean it, she knows. He looks at her and waits for whatever she is about to say or do. When she is silent, he looks out the window, at the city on the brink of another century. It is stark and grey, Orwellian. Yet the hotel room on the thirtieth floor is warm, and last night Fiona had removed her blouse and her bra in a single fluid gesture, as if defying everything. And there was heat in their mouths and bodies which were painted gold by lamplight as if for a circus in France. All that is human was there, even if tonight she suspects his face would be cold if she reached out to touch it. She suspects also that he would flinch if she did, as if she were holding a razor between her thumb and forefinger, poised to slit his cheek.

A long time passes, time enough for her to give him another chance, a chance for him to say something that would include her in his life. She promises herself that if he does, she will not do anything to hurt him after all. The phone starts ringing again; he leaps up from the couch, as if he has been saved.

"Hi, how are you?" he says again. "Yes… yes. I promise, Helen. No, everything's all right. I mean it. Yes, I would… yes. I know. I know that… Look, can I call you back in a minute? A minute. Yes. I'll call you right back."

Raymond puts the phone down and Fiona stands up. She feels she is missing something but she has only brought her purse, which is slung over her shoulder. She is all packaged; it would appear that she has with her everything she needs.

"It sounds like I should leave," she says.

"Yes," he says.

They stand in the middle of the hotel room. She knows that as soon as she walks out the door he will pick up the phone and call his wife. She knows she can make it to the door, down the hall, into the elevator without making a sound. She knows she can do it because that is the strength he gave her when he said I love you to another woman while he turned his back to her and she pressed her lips together until they paled.

Fiona puts her arms around his body. Raymond hugs her as quickly as if she were a stranger, and then pushes her away, stepping back so abruptly she sees her own arms leave his body in a blur, sees how her hand would have curved around his neck but now only grazes his collarbone, sees that hand returning to her side.

She makes it to the door. He shuts it behind her and locks it loudly, the bolt chiming in the silence of the hallway. She makes it down the hall, into the elevator; she walks out into the lobby among the bellhops and businessmen, the married couples and single women. She sees the floral arrangements, the marble surfaces and brass buttons, the glass doors that lead into the wild, dark city in which a taxi will race towards her with its back door springing open. As she heads towards those doors, she hears the sound of high heels on a hard, slick surface. After a moment she realizes it is a sound she is making with her own shoes. It seems incredible to her, that at last she is making a sound.

2.

It was the scent at the back of your neck, where tiny, formed curls sprouted like fiddleheads. That was where it started, that place in your body where I first breathed you into me, gulping you in until I became dizzy and the room circled around me.

The rest of your body revealed itself in stages, in cities where it snowed or rained or the sun was a giant lamp we could not reach up and switch off. The perfect whites of your eyes in which two blue irises gazed upon my face. The contact of your stark white skin, burning against my cheek, before you pushed me away and clasped your hands tight behind your back as if handcuffed. *No. Please go.*

And your flesh, warm and yielding at dawn when I pulled your shirt out of your trousers to rest my face upon your stomach, your breathing keeping me afloat.

The sun stunned your face on the pillow, painted it gold like jewellery on a velvet case in a store window downtown. It seemed to set your hair on fire, and from the bathroom doorway your body swathed in sheets looked as if a tongue of flame was searing you from head to foot in the sudden day.

જી

The night we met, rain was streaking the windows of the yellow taxis pulling up outside the hall where the awards ceremony was being held. Perhaps I knew even then that something was going to change, as the door opened to the sound of laughter and clinking glasses, and I walked in shedding drops of rain on the floor.

Later that evening I stood in front of the women's bathroom, and you appeared at the end of the hall. At that moment you were still, at the top of the stairs with people milling behind you, their glossy mouths closing over the rims of wineglasses. Did you stop to

15

think? You were smiling at me, a slippery smile, inscrutable. I was confused by my reaction, braced against the wall in a swirl of conversation, cigarette smoke and laughter. I looked after you, speechless, as you brushed past.

છ

Two days later, shortly before I flew home, you were helping me into my coat at a hotel bar, and talking about your wife in tones that told me how things were going to be. I knew then that I would sit with you in lounges under chandeliers, never by fireplaces or on living-room couches. There would always be waitresses in long green dresses gliding silently towards our table; men with resentful faces wearing suits and expensive watches; women with jewels hung around their necks and wrists and pushed through their earlobes, with hair cut and styled geometrically, and eyes heavy with paint. Chrysanthemums would flourish under skylights, and liqueurs, flavoured with nuts and oranges and the parched hours after midnight, would swim shallowly in deep glasses. Even though I knew this, I was destroyed. The back of your two fingers against my cheek burned into my skin for days, like a brand of possession.

એ

It was not long before I discovered that all men contained something that reminded me of you. It was the faint scent of their bodies, clean as water; the tender skin around their eyes, like damp, frail violets; the tension of the skin over their cheekbones. It was their full hair under a belt of sunlight, or the way they ran down the street to catch a taxi, their black shoes rising and falling on the pavement, the wind sailing through their suits. During the day I thought of you whenever men walked past me on the street, the permed heads of wives at their shoulders.

When you came to visit me I imagined your skin fresh from the caresses of your wife. I imagined she complained of being cold and that you tucked the blankets around her shoulders as though she were a child and crossed your arms behind her back and held her fiercely close, as you did with me. I saw again the twinned gold bands of the ring on your finger as your hand lay motionless on the white hotel sheets in daylight.

∽

On our first night together here two weeks after we had met, we did nothing but sleep in each other's arms.

In the morning I lay on top of you on the hotel bed, sheets crisp as snow around us, and took one of your hands in mine. There was a full-length mirror on the cabinet at the foot of the bed; I felt you turn your head, unable to resist, to examine our reflections in the glass. What did we look like together, you and I, hotel sheets tumbling around us. Were we viable? Later that day I saw what we looked like when we walked back through the lobby, past glass cases thick with fur coats, studded with jewellery. There were mirrors so polished they glowed green around the edges, and I glanced in one as we approached. We were walking swiftly and I saw only two black suits, my face smiling and turned at an angle towards you. We looked professional and I was briefly shocked that we bore no traces of our transformation in the mirror, that someone could have walked past us, seeing only another couple in that hotel of conventions and assignations.

Nine months later I sat alone in a club close to midnight and thought about you to the pulse of the music. *Say it again. Pain.* The bodies of the boy strippers were pre-adolescent, white as the flesh of cod or sole, gyrating on the stage circled by men. Your body had become as beautiful and ultimately impossible as the bodies of those boys, their feet seeming to flow across the floor, slim-hipped, flat-bellied, their hands so small. Yet as the night wore on I saw that not all the boys were pretty. Some were older, unable to compensate for their aging even with chiselled muscles and a massive bulk inside their coloured panties. One was unattractive; he wore glasses that were thick and opaque beneath the lights. It seemed ridiculous that he was dancing for men who were more attractive than he was, and although he paused in front of each patron to work his hips and pelvis, no one reached out fingers weighted by a folded bill. The boy he was dancing with could not have been more than five feet tall and had a face like a pixie, and he was the one the men loved. They reached slowly as if through water towards the boy's panties, tugging at the string, brushing his satin flesh while slipping the money through. His older partner continued to dance with the sheen of desperation glossing his forehead, making his glasses slip down his face, as he worked earnestly and hopelessly the muscles in his thighs and buttocks.

Men with dipping wrists and the cuffs of their jean jackets turned up passed me in the reddish, smoky dark. Alcohol and fruit juice shot into glasses behind the bar, crashed against ice cubes. The drag queens with their pencilled eyes, cheekbones like the blades of chopping knives, tottered in on strong legs hugged by leather skirts, red, black, candy-floss pink. Their faces were manly, crude, yet made so vulnerable by makeup I thought they would crumple at a touch, their lipstick smearing, their mascara running, their faces screwing up in a howl of pain. It was as if what they had painted onto their faces and tugged over their bodies was a declaration of vulnerability, as if they each possessed inside them a single spot which would detonate when touched. I thought of the night I threatened to handcuff you when I was carrying no handcuffs, had only my body which I pressed desperately against yours as the drag queens pressed their bodies against the unstable bar. Your hair soft as down, your mouth passing between my breasts. The light from the window illuminating your hair and the bottles rattling in the open minibar. The sheets on the bed behind you rumpled like an envelope that had been handled, as you took one nipple and then the other into your mouth. You were on your knees, your hair bright as the first snowfall of the year. Your penis stood against my stomach, pointed as though to bestow a blessing, and the webs of our pubic hair were indistinguishable as shadows merging.

The drag queens wore their quavering, true faces superimposed over the faces beneath. The drag queens didn't yet know how their eyes rimmed in liquid black eye-liner would invite lovers who would want to see those eyes brim with tears, who would strike their hard cheekbones, who would leave them.

Like a child I believed in magic. Like a child I believed when I put my hand between your legs. *Do you love your wife? Yes, I love my wife. Will you still be married to her in ten years? Yes, I think I will, why do you ask? I needed to know. Have you had other affairs? Yes, this is not new, this has happened before.*

We were drinking whisky out of small bottles; each time you uncapped one and handed it to me our fingers touched. They looked like the fingers of children, smooth, blunt. You got up then and drew the curtains, although we were on the fifteenth floor.

(But I have looked out of high-powered antique telescopes in other men's apartments and seen women with matted hair sitting in front of televisions in studios clear across the harbour. I have read the signs of art galleries and Persian rug galleries over the bridge and along the main street. I have seen the rows of word processors and the figures of journalists moving between them in the media building in late-night anonymity. I have focussed the telescope on water and seen it purple and dappled, hazy in its depths, while a man's hands moved along my cold, naked arms.)

Do you love your wife? Yes. Her hair blowing in the faint breeze, across her cheeks, between her lips. Her hair grasped between your hands, stroked across her skull. Her hair fanning across your stomach and between your thighs. You touch her when she does that, when she moves down your body and does that. You rub her temples when she takes you in her mouth and sucks you. You maintain contact. I know this. When I unzipped you I was not prepared for your sudden naked flesh, velvet and sturdy against my hand. With a child's belief in magic I got down on my knees in front of your body. When I put my mouth over your penis above its nest of hair, one moment shifted irrevocably into the next, shifted so hard I thought I heard the sound of something breaking.

The worst thing is obsession, you had said in a lounge with a waterfall falling softly, continuously behind us. You smiled when you said that, drank from your glass. You knew about that one.

Perhaps I was only thinking you would never leave, not after I had done this, even as you were shaking your head, tugging me up, away from your penis which smelled vaguely of sleep, the faintest aura of urine like a perfumed body veil.

I had once tied a man to his bed with lengthy frayed ropes wound between the brass bars. Pushed a ball gag between his teeth, laughed at the blood starting from his nipples. His ankles were so white they seemed tinged with green. Was I thinking about him when I reached over and touched your naked ankle on the coffee table, the intelligent, vulnerable crook of the bone beneath the skin? Did I wonder how your ankle would look bent in black leather, daylight starting in from the window as you lay on the hotel bed, your arms wrested apart from your body and your face poised above your spread-eagled limbs? Would you plead? Would you try to escape? I could imagine you lying so still, your wrists exuding a film of sweat in their leather enclosures. I would come close only to touch your hair, to rest my face upon your chest and hear the rhythm of your heart. I would permit myself only to kiss your neck while I rested my hands on either side of your face, which would be so beautiful it would cause me pain.

I would feel the way the drag queens felt looking upon their impossible lovers, their faces hideously open, their hearts tumbling around behind their great false breasts. *Say it again.* The boys twisting their lupine bodies on the surrounded stage. I would never let anyone hurt you, cause you pain. Your white, attentive face on the pillows barely warmed by the light that flowed into the hotel room, over the chosen furniture. You would always breathe steadily, blink regularly as you watched me rest upon your body. The scent of your body nourishing, alive, as you lay there completely in the moment, your wrists and hands emerging like flares on either side of you, the beautiful bones of your face arranged on the pillow.

Do you love your wife?

I love her.

We kissed in the elevator going down. You looked conservative, contained. I tried to look at you as though you were a stranger. In person you were never as handsome as the composite of features I assembled in my memory during your absences, from men I stood in line with at the drugstore, whom I glimpsed at parties laughing and sipping their drinks, who walked briskly with locked briefcases between the convention rooms of downtown hotels. Yet because you were alive, with a scent and throb to your skin, because your every movement was a miracle of nerve and synapse, an ordering of thought and experience, you were more beautiful inside your body than any idealized image I might have made of you, gone over again and again in my hours of solitude, imbued with the colours of my desire, fondled like a fetish object, a shoe or a glove, representative of its fickle, feared owner. Yet I envied the safety of the fetishist with his charms, his precious life-giving objects, soaked in his beloved's

25

scents. My every passion had come to focus upon you, as the antique telescope focussed upon the woman staring at television in her disordered apartment.

But by day we were ordered people. Look at us in the elevator, descending. The vague outlines of your reflection shone in the brass panelling—your dark blue jacket, your white shirt. It was myself I was unable to see reflected in the dark elevator doors. We separated instantly, with frightening ease, when the elevator stopped on the eleventh floor to fill with a stocky, middle-aged man and a woman wearing a discreetly patterned dress. The remaining descent accompanied by these strangers seemed more awkward than usual, as if they were aware by some perceptive feeling that they had interrupted something, committed some kind of trespass. We stared ahead and did not touch, maintaining a distance between our bodies. You reached up to rub your chin, once, looking at your gold-hued face above the elevator buttons, perhaps suddenly wary of a streak of lipstick, a tell-tale sign.

(One morning I left you with the fresh sunlight flooding the hotel room from the window behind you, left you with a slash of wine-coloured lipstick on your white shirt, above your heart. I knew you would notice it sometime between then and your arrival home—in the bathroom as you packed your toothbrush and razor, in the full-length mirror on the cabinet when you opened it to remove your suit, downstairs or on the plane in the lingering of the concierge's or the stewardess's eye. Even so, I hoped you somehow would not, that you would travel like that the thousands of miles home to your wife, the lipstick clinging to you like a leech, ripe, undisturbed, waiting for the necessary pair of wifely blue eyes to fix there.)

We descended together to our separate vehicles. I watched you leave through two panes of glass—the windshield of my taxi, the back window of your car. Follow that man, I wanted to yell. The one with hair the colour of ashes. Your car described a curve down the driveway in front of the hotel and onto the street. My taxi followed closely behind, the driver oblivious to everything but the gathering cloud and the trips displayed on his monitor. I stared at the back of your head through the panes of glass, as if the sheer force of my gaze would make you cancel your plans for the evening and change the course of your life. Follow that man. The thought made me smile. Of course it was actually very ordinary—two cars, one of them a taxi-cab, for a brief moment on the same street downtown, leaving a busy hotel. Your car slid into another lane and blinked its tail-light as it slowed to turn the corner. The taxi leapt straight ahead, towards the open bridge.

എ

We were always leaving each other. You would raise your hand once before climbing into your car, that risky gesture of acknowledgement, while around us the porters in their jackets with the brass buttons opened doors and swung luggage onto gold-framed racks. The traffic would pass on the street behind you, merging and separating in its dependable pattern, the river of traffic braiding in the street where the store-fronts glittered with initialled leather purses and jew-ellery that lay like faces turned towards the dawn. What was left of the sun would glare for an instant between two clouds and then slip away, as you slipped inside your car and I inside mine, bending our bodies towards our different destinations.

The last time you left it was fall, the streets disappearing under canopies of cindery leaves, a blue sky covering everything. When I first met you, it was spring in another city and it was raining. Never leave me, I often wanted to say to you after that night, but I never did. Instead I would go to the window and look out upon whatever city we had chosen. Rain gurgled in the gutters; sunlight painted bright squares on the walls; branches trembled with leaves or were bare as charcoal sketches of winter. I did not care. I closed my eyes, and in the material dark I breathed against your body in the only hotel room where you were.

3.

In the months following the end of the affair, Fiona spent most of her nights in a bar, looking into the faces of the men around her to see if any of them resembled the man she loved. Sometimes, after several double Scotches, she would find someone who did. There would be a moment when Raymond's remembered features fought with the features of the stranger, and then memory would triumph, and for a little while she would think he had returned. Immediately she would order another drink, trying to sustain the illusion. Being drunk, she felt, was almost as good as having one of those dreams where he was stroking her hair back from her forehead and saying he had made a mistake, he knew now that he loved her, and he was going to leave his wife for her. There was a certain level of intoxication that felt like being inside a dream, and when she felt the protective layers begin to disperse, and light start to intrude, that was when she knew she needed another drink.

But always at some point she would see that the men in the bar resembled him poorly, that if they turned to one side their profiles were entirely dissimilar, or that they were too broad in the waist or shoulders, or that upon closer inspection their faces were lined and the hair on their crowns thinning. And then she would lose that pulse of desire that had begun to beat in her, and she would squeeze between the tables for the exit sign flickering above the stairs. She would realize how smoky and clamorous the bar had been when she had made it out into the street, away from the compressed, milling bodies, the nicotine-coloured air and the neon beer ads sizzling on the walls. Outside it would often be raining, and the air tingling, and the sidewalks hard and glassy. It was a world occupied only by the taxis that slid up and down the road with their lights on and their windshield wipers knocking back and forth in the night.

❧

The days and weeks passed. She could not seem to feel anything except when she drank; when she came home from working in her studio or teaching at the art college, she would go straight to the liquor cabinet. She began to avoid her friends, all of whom were coupled—they represented everything she had hoped for and lost. Sometimes she was convinced that their relationships, too, were built on deception and betrayal, that everyone she knew was committing adultery, or at least harboured fierce, secret obsessions about people outside their marriages. She could not overhear any conversation, witness any event, without relating it to her affair with Raymond.

One night, making an effort, she invited a young married couple over for dinner. She was acquainted with the wife, a sculptor, whom she had met at a gallery opening. The husband was given to enthusiastic gestures as he talked and, during the main course, after he had set down his knife and fork to illustrate with his hands what he was trying to say, he smacked his wedding ring loudly against the glass tabletop.

"Ouch. Oh, sorry," he said, looking at his hand for a moment in disbelief. The ring was still so new on his finger, so recently a part of his body, that he could not protect it the way he might be able to protect himself from stubbing his toe against a coffee table.

Fiona watched them jealously. They were impoverished art school graduates—the husband wore a woollen vest in a Third World pattern, and the wife wore a sweater with shrunken sleeves. They had the thinness and pallor of students, yet their rings weighed their fingers down the way rings weight the hands of wealthy matrons.

જી

Nights that she did not go to the bar, wearing a short skirt and stockings she would later wring out in the bathroom sink, staining the water the colour of suede, she went to the theatre by herself to watch movies about faithless husbands, unconventional "other women," and austere wives who suffered in silence. The scripts were full of clichés, the requisite combinations of love, sex, violence, betrayal. It was always the same story and it felt to her, slumped in a red velvet seat in a theatre that smelled of popcorn and waxy candy, as if it were her story. In some of the scenes the face of the cheating husband became Raymond's face—the shape of his mouth as it traced the outline of his mistress's breast, the way he drew in his breath and flinched when his wife slapped his face, all his moral confusion. She would leave the theatre in tears, stumbling into the downtown street busy with teenagers and buses.

Once she was home she would realize again that she had nothing left over from their relationship. There was nothing to fetishize—no letters, lost buttons, half-smoked cigarettes. One humid evening over a year ago, she had worn a pale linen dress which had become suffused with their mingled scents. The next day she wondered if she should take it to the dry-cleaner's, if she should not instead keep their body smells joined for as long as possible in the loosely woven fabric. But she had resisted what she saw as an indication of a sickness in her, the first hint of a darkness she did not want to explore, and so she took it in. When the dress was returned to her in a transparent bag, smelling slightly, sourly, of dry-cleaning fluid, every wrinkle had been pressed out; it

was flat and blank as paper on which nothing had
ever been written.

෨

Fiona resolved to stop drinking, take a holiday, break
the pattern by going somewhere new. One weekend,
six months after the last time she had seen Raymond,
she packed a bag, booked a bus ticket and made a
reservation for the hotel room with the best view in a
resort a few hundred miles across the border.

It was not what she expected. The town was pop-
ulated by couples wearing matching sweatshirts and
tennis shoes. It was not yet the height of the season,
and many of the restaurants and tourist shops were
still closed. The cafés had plastic flowers on the tables,
and the gift shops sold clumsily carved jade jewellery,
minerals polished to look like precious stones, and
pricey boxed chocolates.

But since she was here, she was determined to
have her holiday. She resisted the miniature bottles of
liquor in the minibar, limiting herself to hamburgers
and Banana Daquiris ordered from room service. She
tried to read, but his face would swim into view above
the cluttered pages of novels and story collections.

She walked around and around the cobbled streets of town, pretending to admire the merchandise. In one clothing store she watched as a woman in her fifties, wearing severe eye makeup and a bouffant hairstyle, plucked a white bathing suit off the rack and held it up against her body.

"You have a white suit just like it at home," her husband said, inching towards the door.

"No, I don't," the woman said, "this is different."

"How is it different?"

"It just is," she said angrily, "it's different."

"Oh, okay, I'm sorry," he said mollifyingly. "You're right. This one's sort of cream, not white."

"Oh?" she said.

"Yes," he said, trying to be helpful, "the cream lining inside, it shows through the material of the bathing suit and makes it look darker."

"I didn't notice that," the woman said. She replaced the suit on the rack, and the couple walked back outside.

Fiona ate some of her meals in restaurants with nappy red carpets on the floor, velvet paintings on the walls, and perfectly shaped electric flames jumping in the fireplace. She sipped cocktails from recycled glass-ware whose stems were still hot from the dishwasher. Once she sat at a table next to a balding man in shorts and a golf T-shirt, and a woman who wore blue eye-shadow and fuchsia lipstick. "But, sweetie," the woman kept saying in a cloying, manipulative tone, "but, darling, listen to me. No, no, come on, honey, that's not true," and, more insistently, "But under-stand, dear, you've got to understand how I feel," while the man grunted, shook his head, and swore under his breath.

All around her Fiona saw these tableaus of in-volvement. They were highlighted in the quiet resort town; any human interaction took on a greater significance than it would have had she stayed in the city. Sometimes she pretended Raymond was with her and that they were together on holiday—something that had never been a possibility during their relation-ship. She would talk to him under her breath while crouched on the empty shore, snapping pebbles onto the water's surface, composing her face and smiling whenever someone came up the path. She would make subtle faces at him across tables-for-two in cafés

and restaurants—winking knowingly, lifting her eyebrows sarcastically—while eavesdropping on the conversations of the diners around her.

In the evenings the lamps outside the hotel were
lit, and reflected like harvest moons off the surface of
the lake. The wind picked up, and insects buzzed
blackly in the air. The smell of freshwater shrimp,
strong as the odours from a restaurant, drifted up
from the depths of the lake and into the town. She
wrapped a bathrobe around herself and padded barefoot through the hotel hallways, past the clank and
gurgle of ice machines and pop dispensers, down past
the lobby and to the whirlpool spa located at the centre of the hotel. There she would sit in her bathing
suit, watching the hands turn on the clock. She
shared the whirlpool with people of varying ages, all
with unfashionable bodies—older men who lowered
their wrinkled torsos carefully into the water, aware of
the fragility of their bones; fat middle-aged women
whose bathing suits billowed around their breasts and
thighs. Everyone gave each other tight polite smiles,
then leaned back with sighs of pleasure or self-con-
scious giggles. She stared down at their limbs col-

lected in the sucking, gorging water. Their body parts made her think of movies she'd seen, movies about men who were obsessed with women, or vice versa, who stalked them and chopped them up when they could not have them whole. It made some sense to her now.

After her soak in the whirlpool Fiona rode the elevator back up to her room. The balcony doors opened upon a perfect stillness crimped at the edges by the shuffling of the lake upon the foot of the shore. In this suffocating calm she lay awake on the king-sized bed, and her thoughts of Raymond gathered into a physical pain in her chest, a searing fist planted above her heart. But when she did finally slip, almost accidentally, into sleep, it was to dream about her parents. It had always been this way—the two people she managed to ignore in her waking hours still controlled her nocturnal world. But now her dreams about the family she had left behind were confused with her longing for Raymond, which grafted itself upon the familiar scenes of her childhood—her mother screaming, her father leaving. Only now her father's face was Raymond's, and her mother wore the same clothes Fiona had worn the night she met the man she loved.

ço

On her way back home, as the bus approached the border, the driver asked everyone to disembark at the duty station with their baggage and passports. The passengers filed off the bus, blinking into the washed blue midnight, irritable and nervous. The station was furnished with orange plastic chairs, fluorescent lights; the guard at the desk waved each person over with a contemptuous flick of his fingers. When it was Fiona's turn he glanced at her passport and waved her through. She did not look like a woman who had anything to hide.

But he stopped another woman from the bus, would not let her past.

"What do you do for a living?"

"I'm a writer."

"What kind of a writer?"

"I write stories, poems… I'm working on a novel."

"Let me see your bags."

The writer had dry, limp hair and meagre hips, and she wore army-issue clothing. She was carrying three canvas bags full of manuscripts which she had not let anyone touch. Now the border guard began to lift the manuscripts onto a conveyor belt while she paced, brushed her hair off her forehead, scowled. She ended her answers to his questions with loud, protracted sighs, which sounded sarcastic.

"What the hell is the matter with you?" the guard said.

He called out to another guard and together they began tearing the elastics from the manuscripts and examining each page. There must have been thousands of pages. The writer crossed her arms over her chest and stood gazing over her exposed work.

The other passengers filtered back to the bus and watched with interest the activity inside the lit station. "Maybe they think she's writing pornography," someone speculated.

"Haven't they changed the censorship laws recently?" someone else asked.

"Be careful what you write!" another person admonished, to no one in particular.

"She shouldn't be so surly, she'd get off a lot easier if she would just be nice," a man reasoned.

"Yeah, and then we could get this bus moving," said a teenager.

An hour later the bus driver emerged from the station and climbed aboard, starting the engine without any explanation. The writer was being left behind at the border. All the passengers were curious as to her fate but it seemed bad taste to show so much interest in another's misfortune, so no one said anything.

Fiona felt surprised and lucky that she had made it so easily across the border. Then she remembered that she was returning to the country of her birth, and that she had had nothing to declare.

⁊

A month after her holiday, an exhibition of her work took Fiona to the city where Raymond lived. She would only be there for four days, and most of her time would be taken up by interviews and talks she was expected to give about her work. Still, she found time to see some people she had met on previous trips, who offered to take her to a variety of restaurants and nightspots. She always chose restaurants she thought Raymond might be dining in. She knew he favoured trendy, pricey establishments where the food was arranged sparingly on huge octagonal plates; she sat miserably through several such meals, picking at food that seemed elastic and oily, looking for him seated at the bar, or in a booth with men and women still in their office clothes, or out on a terrace with his wife or another woman.

One evening she was asked to dinner by a group of people she was expected to impress—curators, buyers, executives from corporations that invested in up-and-coming artists. The restaurant where they were meeting for dinner had opened only weeks ago; it had melon-coloured walls, pillars in the centre of the long room, and mirrors shaped like sunbursts radiating above the heads of the diners. The *maître d'* was engagingly flustered, there was a line-up at the door, and first reviews decorated the entrance. At the other tables the men wore white shirts and olive slacks; the women wore skimpy vests that showed off their thin, sculpted arms.

Fiona was already a little tipsy when she arrived. She had not wanted to draw attention to herself during dinner by ordering too much to drink, so she had quickly downed two whiskys from the hotel minibar before hailing a taxi. But when one of the men at her table ordered a Scotch before dinner, she did too. Suddenly she wanted to reach that level of intoxication that made her feel as intensely alive as she used to feel around Raymond; she thought that if she could drink herself back inside that space, she would find him there, waiting, ready to give her another chance.

By the time the entrées arrived she was drunk and no longer hungry. She found it an effort keeping track of the conversations at the table, and she had forgotten the names of the men and women seated around her. The man beside her had a pleasant face and silver-rimmed glasses; he wore a sombre suit. She found herself touching his hands or his sleeve for emphasis, whispering into his ear. With a surge of shame she realized that she was flirting openly with him, and that he was looking at her with a mixture of interest and suspicion, like someone keeping the chain on a door opened to a stranger.

"Yes, I'm married," he said, in answer to a question she could not remember asking. "We have four kids."

The plates were cleared, orders for dessert and coffee taken. She asked for a brandy, although her head was swimming and the sorbet colours of the restaurant hurt her eyes. She tried to persuade the man to drink with her, but he shook his head. "I really can't," he said. "I brought my car, and I'm working tomorrow." She felt that she had somehow failed then, and she drank the brandy from its snifter as though it were wine, and asked for another. Outside it had started to rain, and once the sky was cracked by tender white filaments of lightning. She spilled some brandy on her blouse, and thought she saw the people around her averting their eyes as she dabbed clumsily at herself with a wet napkin.

When the bill was paid, everyone stood to go, the men shaking hands, the women kissing each other on the cheeks. Fiona turned to the man beside her.

"I've wanted to do this all evening," she said, and reached up to touch his face. Instead of touching her back, instead of smiling invitingly and looking at her with lust, he gazed at her gravely; the caution and pity in his eyes made her wish she were dead.

∽

On the morning of her last day in the city where Raymond lived, the sky was nearly white above the office towers downtown. Summer was coming. Businessmen stood on street corners talking on cellular phones and waiting for the lights to change; women in smart suits and sensible shoes strode out of coffee bars with their lattes and espressos. A bike courier pedalled alongside the curb, the muscles on his legs violently delineated; a teenaged girl rollerbladed down the sidewalk, her midriff gleaming beneath her cropped T-shirt. Fiona was in a taxi headed for the airport, hungover, when suddenly the driver turned a corner and she saw for the first time the building where Raymond worked.

It was an ordinary office tower, sharp-angled, sheathed in glass, like any other in the downtown core. She thought she would catch only a glimpse of it as they drove past, but then she heard trumpets, and the merging traffic slowed between lanes, and the driver shifted into neutral. Their taxi was stopped right in front of Raymond's building.

"Shit. Can you believe this? It's a parade. It's a fucking *parade*. I hope your flight isn't leaving before noon."

"It isn't," she said, bemused. The sound of trumpets grew louder, and then a phalanx of marchers, both children and adults, came down the middle of the street from around the corner of his building. They were wearing tights and tassels, and bashing cymbals, and blowing horns; they were followed by floats sparkling with tinsel and lights, ambling down the road like giant cakes, topped by women in aprons who swung their hips and called out words she could not understand above the confusion of instruments and the bellows from the bull-horns at the edges of the parade.

"What's going on?" she asked.

"Oh, I don't know, crazy shit like this happens all the time. Crazy city. Needs a new government, if you ask me. Who knows, it's some anniversary or Jewish holiday or something... no, wait. That banner there, 'In Celebration of the Year of the Family.' See, I knew it was some government crap."

Fiona leaned back in her seat, rolling her own window down as far as it would go, drinking in the noise and the daylight. A few feet away, across the sidewalk, was the entrance to the place where Raymond worked. The brushed steel columns in front of the door looked like they might be cold to the touch. She closed her eyes and let the discordant sounds flood her senses. For the first time, she felt something—a bright leaking inside her—that might be hope, or at least an indication of something changing ahead. When she looked up at Raymond's building she thought she saw him standing at one of the windows, lured there by the noise in the street below. She wasn't sure. It could have been anyone, and by then the traffic was moving again.

4.

Two weeks before the end of our affair, I had come to California to stand on a famous street corner and think of you. It was raining hot as the tears of a child's tantrum on the boulevard, and the lights of the twenty-four-hour liquor stores were my only direction back to my hotel. I began to walk down the block, fitting my feet into the footprints of dead stars who had fumbled anxious and bored in presidential hotel suites decades before. I walked the length of the dying boulevard whispering your name, but you did not come. Already you had named your wife and called her your love, your safe harbour.

Once again, months after you left me, the plane

begins its descent into Los Angeles, into what I first think is darkness. But when I look out the windows on the other side of the aircraft, I see along one edge of the city the sunset bleeding its *maquillage* colours, its commercially duplicated crimsons and mandarins. The colours go brighter and brighter as we land.

౪

It is winter but outside the house the day is a foggy blue fantasy of warmth, the air weighty and tropical, medicinal as eucalyptus. I lie in bed listening to the sound of police helicopters circling the sky, low and wide, searching for criminals. The helicopters circle like dreams, concentric, one overlapping another until I am fully awake. I am staying in a room behind closed blinds, with a jug of wildflowers on a desk by the bed. Upstairs my friend Jessica sleeps in a black bed, and her bathroom is a sea of mirrors and pots of makeup like wave-washed stones, flint and rose quartz, flung upon the beach. Her roommate Kyle, an actor, is already at the breakfast table drinking orange juice, reading the hefty paper, wearing a winter cap with ear flaps bent down in readiness for a morning audition for a weekly television series. A few minutes later there are gunshots in the neighbourhood, and Jessica and Kyle glance uneasily towards the windows. They do not see anything, but they know that outside something is happening.

In the morning Jessica and I drive along many boulevards, through the spice-smelling hills, down endless liquid freeways. When I lean out the car window my face becomes coated with a fine film of dust and pollution. After lunch we visit a sex shop where, beneath the glass counter, there is a real life replica of a vagina, the black hairs on the nether lips curling like sea foam, connected to a funnel through which the semen can run out. I wonder if you have ever come here with your wife, to this store which is as gorgeous and shameless as a voluptuous woman wearing inappropriate clothing. Romance is bottled row on row upon the shelves, among boxes of condom lollipops, suckers shaped like genitals, porn videos in packages gilded as antique novels. I remember how in a hotel room in my city by the sea, above a parking lot and a rose garden, once and once only, you held my hand and we watched a night of ordinary television. We both said we disliked pornography. We agreed the best scenes in the movie we were watching were the interior shots. We sighed simultaneously, we both wore white. I wanted to touch the tip of my tongue to the scar on your knuckle, to be unable to speak for days.

"You like violent movies?"

"I love them."

"Well here, in last week's LA Times, I saw an ad for one." You threw the paper into my lap like a great unwieldy bird with fanning wings. *"See if you can find it. If you can, we'll go to the city and see it together…"*

Of course you did not say that last sentence. But it was understood, an unspoken promise, like the many to which we held each other. I looked and looked under all the listings, I promise I did, but I am now sitting alone in a café overlooking a parking lot off the avenue, among many women frozen into their youth, their greatest asset, wearing bracelets and chokers and earrings but no symbols of their sexual fidelity to others. I watch women walk to their cars carrying glossy bags, their legs stretching like colts', their faces closed as night flowers. I think of your wife. I think of your fingers resting on her pulse, judging her response, measuring the pace by which she lives; I think of the two of you in this town walking together, your shoulders occasionally touching like twins. She is what you have chosen, in the end; she is all that there is.

I grow so busy thinking about you that, when I get up to leave, I walk right past a famous actress who is gazing out upon the same parking lot through eyes like chunks of crystal.

"Oh, take a pill," a woman in a dominatrix-black outfit spits at the man she is with as they emerge from the juice bar holding their freshly squeezed drinks, out onto the terrace overlooking the lot. "It's hard to find women here," a man in a security guard uniform says to the woman at the next table, whose feet are hidden by a red sea of parcels. The famous actress says nothing; she has hair as blond as a Finn, and a body built for suits of leather and spandex. I wonder how many people I have walked past in the last year, thinking only of you.

ඏ

These are days of health clubs and strip malls, the parking lots as falsely cheerful as car dealerships, flags in the country's colours draping the lots like a beauty contestant's ribbons. As Kyle and I leave the car and walk to the gym I see the advancing army of worked-out bodies hoisting gym bags and weight belts, their bellies striated with muscle. The parking lot shimmers in the heat, and the flags hang still in the absence of breeze. Once, as if in penitence for a moment of infidelity, you spent hours at the gym, became ill, submitted yourself to painful dentistry... *There is nothing of me left*, you said, *I am not alive.* Your muscles glowed white in the discreetly darkened hotel room.

The gym is a multi-levelled monstrosity in which a thousand members pump and press, anxious to exchange their given bodies for others. All about me, reflected tenfold, are the grimaces of near achievement, kneecaps bicycling, the dimpling of working muscles. Women whose gasping faces emerge from the waves of the pool appear in that moment of rising as featureless as amoeba; their black Lycra-clad hips travel easily through water; later they lie curled upon towels with their faces turned to the walls as if in defeat or shame. Two men battle in the resounding prison of the squash court, and pouty-faced young women wait by the juice bar for their lovers whose inflated bodies lumber inside the advanced weight room, prehistoric, among weights the colour of iron and stone.

The gym is a country unto itself, a land of mirrors and pink fluorescent tubing, television monitors fastened to the wall upon which while exercising we fix our imploring eyes as if on lovers as they are leaving. A storm is approaching the southern states, the anchorwoman in her bright blazer announces. Off in the distance, black clouds boil. And more rapes and more deaths, the mug shots of the men on screen so like those of the men in the next lane on the freeway, in the flow of traffic, staring back at me with eyes that signal nothing.

We race on our sophisticated computerized bicycles, but nothing really moves. All is stationary; we run and climb always in the same place where we would be still. I descend the staircase into another section of the gym, only to be greeted by my own self in the mirror waiting below. I enter one room after another deceptive with mirrors; for all I know it might be the same room; I exist everywhere at once and at the same time I am lost, I do not find any trace of my history in the face and body that caresses shining weights, that moves as repetitiously as a trained machine, that is absent of the dimension of intelligence in these mirrors that show only my prepared physical self and nothing of what lives beneath. Is it any wonder that we flock here as if to Mecca, that the parking lot can barely contain the thousands that arrive at this gym daily in their gleaming, empty-eyed multitudes? In my own way I am searching for you here, you who have waited at the bottom of a staircase for a woman to descend trailing white, you whose skin is as reflective as any mirror. Here I lose myself as much as I am ever able, drowning in the aerobic instructor's galvanizing cries as he dances onto the stage, music pulsing like a heart under strain. The mirror tells me I am acceptable though not special, and I welcome the mirror's annihilating verdict, my safe disappearance into the reflected horde. Kyle and I spend hours in the factory of bodies, watching sweat spread along collar-bones and shoulder-blades. Is escape to be found at last in the endorphin surge, the digital Congratulations that blinks on the machine's monitor upon completion of a programmed set? I rise pumping feverishly into a dream of white dresses, glittering night freeways and a vision of your wife touching her lips once, quickly, to the side of your face.

౫

In the clothing stores I try on dresses and twist in front of mirrors but see only with the albumen eyes of the blind. I see myself in a wedding dress crumpled and stained; black buttons decorate my breast. I hold a fistful of dead red roses, brittle as dried bloodstains, and walk through incense so thick it leaves a trail of ashes across my gown. Outside on the trendy avenue handsome young men with movie-star hair pin adolescent girls dressed like prostitutes to the walls of fashion boutiques and hamburger joints where lazy neons blink. A group of Asian girls gingerly smokes cigarettes outside a sex shop, their faces resentfully virginal. The river of youth passes, its fashions changing season to season. Black bands, as if of mourning, around magnolia necks; lipstick dark as theatrical makeup. These girls are conscious of themselves as part of a parade to which eyes are irresistibly drawn, yet their sexual bodies betray no knowledge of sex,

57

none of the instinctive compelling rhythms. They are poor actors after all, dressed for the part but bereft of lines, and they stand garishly upon the street's stage, as striking as gargoyles.

The morning papers are filled with beautiful men and women looking for each other in the classifieds, but somehow day after day they continue to miss each other as I miss you among the faces that pass on the steaming avenue, blank faces not yet stamped with pain and the scourge of isolation, that betray no conflict and no loyalty. I sit under a heat lamp tall as a palm tree in front of a restaurant built of chrome and neon, away from the girls and boys at the counter who admire their hair in each reflective surface provided. Women slink down the street, swinging small crochet purses. They have attained the impossible, they will never age. A hundred years from now they will still be here, in the bodies of other women possessing their exact chemical combinations of boredom, vanity and insecurity, and behind them will always be the men in their costly cars, one hand resting carelessly on the steering wheel, their eyes flaring briefly with the greed of consumers.

Your wife does not look like a woman of this city. Her sweetly shaped lips, the expression lines around her eyes, the breadth of the wrinkles that cut horizontally across the lap of her skirt when she rises. Yet I watch for her, too, to come down the avenue, out of the mini malls, the avaricious storefronts, the laundromats and 7-Elevens, the porn shops with their childishly proud displays of cards, T-shirts and flavourful gels... *He was like candy in my mouth*, one card reads... Yes, it was her husband who was like candy in my mouth, whose reflection I sought in the city's gym among its cast of thousands.

The next day Jessica and I tour store after store, the sweet smells of expensive chemicals in glass vials, roses swimming in flasks full of liquid smooth as amber or honeysuckle, roses like fetuses suspended in brine, pickled and staring from the stores' shelves. We run our fingers along racks of clothing like the pages of books, selecting the images we wish to retain, at least for a while. I wake from a daydream tasting your skin white and cold as the snow blanketing an iceberg. It is this that no avenue of palms, no glass-fronted designer stores and impulsive purchases can replace.

When I turn in a store's mirror wearing a new skirt it is you I intend to consult, and instead I find Jessica asking for assistance with the zipper on a dress she is trying on. Even as, somewhere, your hand rests on your wife's sandy back, I finish zipping my friend and she lets loose her fall of hair to admire and criticize herself in the store's silent mirror.

ひ

The weekend streets at night are wound with neon, and the lanes of traffic heading in opposite directions flash like silver fish in black water. We pass parks where the bodies of young hookers were discarded and, recently, have begun to be discarded again. In the back seat one of Jessica's Hollywood acquaintances, a Beverly Hills matron who is our mothers' age, tells of her husband's infidelity.

"I married him twice," she says, "the first time I left because he was running around on me, and I could not stand that."

Her eyes are wide with makeup in the visor mirror, her roseola-afflicted skin smoothed into stone by the night's application of foundation. Her voice blurs as we gain another freeway, picking up speed; her bangs blow off her forehead in a neat round curl.

"Did you still love him when you left?" I ask.

"Well, I did go back," she says. "I married him again. Now I make him buy me presents on both anniversaries."

"Will he cheat on you again?"

"I don't think so. I own half the house and he loves his house too much to risk losing it."

"Is that all? Is that all that's keeping him from cheating?"

"He loves his house," she repeats. "I am more apt to run around on him, now."

In the café over dinner I notice the lines that form under her eyes when she smiles, the minute cracks in her makeup, I see the faint spots of age on her skin so thin it barely contains her. A wife. The other diners are noisy beneath the high ceilings, the prints of pigs and angels on the walls. Tables of men glance over at us—a table of women—between their bites of food, as if we are television. Once when I look up from my plate I think I see you, walking in after the valet has driven your car away, stepping behind a girl with lank blond hair and red lips who looks nervously in every direction. My heart seizes. That hair, that set of the mouth that has pressed upon my own. Yet the man is a stranger, after all, and our eyes never meet. Laughter and conversation rise over the moment and make it disappear. *Happy birthday to you*, a waitress sings, cupping the flame of a candle set into a cupcake as she carries it to a table by the window, and the restaurant lights flash and dim, and another waiter lights a sparkler and twirls it round, and gamely all the diners join in singing, clapping for the celebrant they cannot even see over the crowded tables.

Later in the night we find our way into a black-walled club where a grinning skeleton slumps over the bar, and men and women stand shoulder to shoulder as they would at a successful party, and the names of exotic drinks are called out to the bartender—White Carnation, Rusty Nail, Strawberry Margarita. We stay here until two a.m. when the glasses are collected, when nothing of our presence remains, and we stumble into the frozen air embracing ourselves, and turn and turn again in our vehicle along the canyon roads, sober with cold, down into the Valley and sleep.

❦

On the boardwalk on my last day here, nothing remains of the night. The crowds are fantastic as a carnival, and Jessica and I wander from store to store, buying cheap muscle shirts and beaded earrings, part of the parade. Incense blows a thick breeze from store entrances, and conflicting strains of opera, Top 40 and Golden Oldies blast from benches and sidewalk cafés and under sheltering palms. A young homeless woman in stained sweatpants meanders among the hand-holding couples, tugging at her waistband, somehow betrayed by her slim, toned body with its winter tan which speaks of the vacations of the wealthy. The sea is separated from the boardwalk by a long border of sand, parts of which have been raised to form rock-like boulders by the press and suck of the tide, but which crumble under my weight. The sand nearest the water is washed into a latex layer of blue, and the water runs in like a shirred skirt, and the surf pounds beneath the sun. On the pier I sit beside a man listening to the baseball scores from his radio, and watch another man walk below us towards the water with his girlfriend, letting go of her hand to mimic a body-builder's stance, arms and legs peculiarly cocked, face tilted as if to display a profile chiselled from rock. He drops the pose, takes her hand again. She is laughing; they are quite ordinary.

Back on the boardwalk, a legless black man sits on a skateboard in front of a stereo, twisting to the music, his arms flapping, his face fixed into a grotesque parody of joy. *Do you love me...* Further down, a big-bellied woman in sloppy pants and a bikini top shakes a rattle and gestures at the person behind her who is wearing a purple dinosaur costume, complete with horned tail and clumsy hands and a mouth black and wide as sorrow. "Come on up, don't be shy, get your picture taken with Barney," she calls over and over, shaking her old rattle, while the world passes by and her only interested customer is a mixed-race boy, who clutches the dinosaur's legs in recognition and love. Women wheel their babies past, indifferent to the woman's cries, her dusty desert-brown hair falling over and over across her face like a lover's slaps.

The ocean glitters its prizewinning ribbon the length of the beach, and a kite hangs for a moment in the air, sharp as a bat's wing, before swooping out of sight. Children totter past in overalls or shorts and T-shirts, eating churros, Mexican fried pastries dipped in a thick layer of sugar that lines their lips and spills down their clothes, sparkling like angel dust. Groups of young men stop groups of girls wearing jeans and tank tops: "So, what are you ladies up to today?" they ask with their already suave, untrustworthy voices. "Oh, just walking around," they reply in high, giggly tones, already teasing, already withdrawing.

Your skin is so cold, I had said wonderingly once in a hotel room where we sat facing each other, kissing and drawing back, where fear and passion leapt between us like a wall of fire. *I am cold,* you said, *you'll learn that about me eventually.* Laughing. *No, no,* I'd insisted, searching for your heat with my fingers, my tongue, certain of its existence under your snowy skin like a hibernating animal's, and never did I question when I could not find it, when all night I tried to warm your body yet you woke at dawn with your drained face and your wedding band pulsing brightly as blood.

This is what I remember now, in the middle of

the boardwalk in the middle of the tropical winter afternoon. I remember your mouth, its pliancy, its memory, how well it matched the movements of my own, gentle and hurtful, exploratory and shy. It has been two years since we first met, since I first felt myself changed by love. *I love my wife*, you had said then. For a moment you were quiet, thoughtful, and then you looked up at me with eyes that were fierce and far away. *I do love her. I do.*

On the lengthy drive back to her home in the Valley, my girlfriend and I do not talk about love. We find other things to say, other things to fill the silence that sometimes comes up between people when they have been together, and close, for a long time.

5.

Fiona thinks she will put up with any conditions to be near Raymond, the first man for whom she has felt this confusion of desire. To kneel in front of him, to take him in her mouth and glimpse between her lowered lashes his head flung back against the back of the couch in her apartment, his face and throat silver in the glow of the streetlight through the window, his expression concentrated inward upon pleasure.

"Why am I doing this?" she had asked at first, her cheek against his thigh.

"Don't do it then, if you don't know," he said softly, motionless, and she shook her head and continued, because it was what she wanted to do.

Now she seeks his body as though it is a source of sustenance. His skin is as white as marble and full of scent. When she drowses with her arms clasped around him and her hair tumbled across his stomach, she matches the rhythm of her breathing to his until she feels there is no longer anything separating them.

They have been seeing each other for almost a year; she still does not know his home phone number, and when she calls his office she uses another name. "This is Iris Cleary," she says in a detached, business-like voice. "Yes, he'll know what it's regarding." Sometimes his secretary puts her through as soon as she gives this name which is not her own, so that suddenly Raymond is no longer in a meeting or away from the building, but just as often she is added to his list of messages. The walls which keep out his business enemies have the added effect of excluding the woman with whom he says he feels completely vulnerable.

Then Raymond goes on holiday with his wife to celebrate their fifteenth wedding anniversary. "I'll think of you," he says; she does not ask him to say anything more. But it is during this time that Fiona starts waking at four in the morning, always after the dream where Raymond is standing at the end of a corridor that slopes downwards; behind him is the opening that leads into the belly of an airplane. She is running towards him from the other end of the corridor, shouting his name and some words too—it seems he has forgotten to give her something important. Upon hearing her he turns and opens his hands without lifting them; he raises the palms to show that they are empty. Already the wind outside the terminal is tugging at his hair, lifting it in lustrous waves so that it blows like a flag. He is wearing colours she has never seen on him before, not his usual black suits and gray cashmere sweaters, but browns and greens, the colours of the earth. A stewardess appears behind him to guide him into the plane. When Fiona wakes, always at the same instant, always just before he turns and walks on board—she can see him starting to turn, the twist in his shoulders, there is never any question he is going to leave—it is with the feeling that everything alive in the world is leaving with him.

Fiona grows used to the way the city sounds at four in the morning—the settling of the leaves in the trees in the neighbourhood, a breeze like an exhalation of breath, the thin, scratchy singing of a solitary bird. She lies in bed until this is no longer bearable, then she paces the moonlit living-room floor. She feels as if her body is on fire, as if she is burning up without him. Four a.m. is a suspended hour, full of darkness yet with a detectable glow that lies waiting inside it, ready to bloom the way electric lights soon will in bedrooms and kitchens while husbands and wives wake and prepare for the day's work. It takes a while for the sky to lighten, and Fiona is exhausted by the time it does.

She does not know how other people have affairs and manage simultaneously to go on with their lives. Often by mid-morning she feels as if she has already completed her work, in the battleground of sleep and the effort of rising. From her office at the art college where she teaches, she goes directly to the gym where, with her hair tied back and sweat spreading between her breasts, she races on stationary bikes and climbs digital hills on Lifecycles. The beat of the music is obsessive, and around her women's limbs flex through one set of exercises after another. "Four! Three! Two! One!" the aerobics instructor shouts between clenched teeth, lips stretched in a perpetual grin. There Fiona thinks about Raymond and recalls how he smiles at her, slightly more with one corner of his mouth than the other, and how it feels when he holds her hand and laces their fingers together as if they are teenagers and in love.

She also thinks of the time he cried recently when he was with her, the tight sobs forced up past his throat like water travelling a long way up through a crack in layers of stone.

"I can't leave her," he said in the darkness that had entered her apartment. His face was chalky, his agitated fingers stroked her own damp cheek. "Please don't ask that of me."

☙

In the evenings Fiona sits in her studio, bags of junk food and photographs of his wife Helen spread out on the desk in front of her. She clips the photos out of business magazines and newspapers where profiles of Raymond appear; most are publicity shots, but some were taken at receptions and dinners where Helen was at her husband's side. One after another, Fiona tears open packages of cream-filled cookies and sugared donuts, conveying the contents almost robotically to her mouth; she studies the photos until her neck tightens and a throbbing starts in her temples.

She thinks she knows what it is like to live inside Helen's body, wearing her clothes, that designer sweater with the gold buttons, that white suit. She can feel against her own skin the barbed caress of the cashmere sweater, the cooler, liquid sensation of the suit. There is no doubt that her lover's wife, approaching middle age, is still an attractive woman. She wears plum lipstick and has straight light hair that frames her heart-shaped face. Her eyes are slightly downcast in the outer corners, lending her an air of sadness and introspection.

Fiona lingers the longest over a recent photograph in which Raymond and Helen are standing at the head table in a hotel ballroom, either about to sit down or to applaud the evening's speaker. Their faces are tilted back a little, suggesting to Fiona that they are looking up at someone at a podium. This photograph was taken only hours after Raymond had come to see Fiona in her apartment. Yet there is nothing about his face or the way he stands that indicates he has recently been intimate with anyone other than his wife. They stand easily beside each other, and Fiona thinks she sees between them a comfort and a love that will last. There is nothing awkward about their pairing, nothing staged. She recognizes in their faces and bodies the looks of two people who will remain attractive into their retirement, who will grow to resemble the couples in life insurance commercials, with crisp silver hair and laugh lines radiating from their eyes.

Fiona stares at this photograph until it dissolves into black and white particles, the grain of the newsprint exposed. Nausea rises in a sour wave inside her as she searches Raymond's face for some evidence of their affair, not knowing exactly what she is looking for but expecting it to be there—a small bruise, a hint of lipstick, the crescent shapes of her fingernails on the backs of his hands. But his body betrays nothing; he is smiling quite cheerfully, and his wife is smiling too, her burgundy lips parted over her teeth. Yet hours before this picture was taken Fiona had bit his mouth while they were kissing, her shoulder-blades pushed back against the bedroom wall and his hands on her upper arms, bit him hard enough that he released her and leapt back, exclaiming. She laughed and drew her finger gently along his hurt lip; he approached her again, cautiously, and she kissed him softly then, holding his lower lip between hers as if it might burst if she exerted more pressure.

"Sometimes you hurt me," he told her once, gravely. What he does not know is that any pain she gives him is not out of her rising excitement, but because she is trying to leave a mark upon him. That is why she bites his mouth as if to draw blood, to break the skin's elastic surface and taste his opened flesh. That is why she buries her face, her breasts in his hair, leaving it scented and unruly. She wants only to leave some mark of her passing on his body, so she can point to it later in a photograph and say, I did that, I was a part of this man's life. Because Raymond has been careful from the beginning, leaving her not so much as a handwritten note in the time they have been together, she has nothing to prove he loves anyone other than the woman at his side, whose smooth hair and gold jewellery reflect the light.

Fiona can no longer trust anything in the media, not even the photographs, not when Raymond can smile out from the pages of a newspaper without even a shadow across his face. It makes her dizzy to think of all the private lives teeming behind those who are in the public eye—the real lives of the men with their wives, their families, their mistresses, and also their interior lives that not even someone close to them can fathom.

When the dizziness and the nausea overwhelm her, she goes to the bathroom and kneels in front of the toilet, bringing up the forbidden foods she has consumed in sweet, doughy lumps. It hurts when she does this, and sometimes she hugs the rim of the toilet and cries, but afterwards as she splashes water on her face and brushes her teeth she feels cleansed, some of the pressure inside her released. She feels ready to return to the photographs and, her stomach empty again, what remains of the food.

Back in the studio Fiona touches the image of Raymond's face with her fingertips, traces the line of his tuxedo. He looks perfectly in the moment, as if he has already forgotten the afternoon, as if he is only listening to the words issuing from the podium, the clatter of glasses, and feeling his wife's presence at his side. Fiona wishes she had bit him so hard his lip had split and blood had trickled spongily into her own mouth. She wishes that in the photograph he winces as he smiles, a gash in his lower lip attracting the reader's eye—is it just a smudge on the newspaper, a spill of ink?—and that his wife stands stiffly and is also finding it hard to smile. She wants them to look pained, valiant, disrupted like people desperately straightening themselves out to face the public after a private battle. But to look at them as they are in the papers makes Fiona feel as if she does not exist; in the public's perception of what is real, she does not.

సం

On weekends when Fiona goes running she passes couples on the street going about their Saturday afternoon business. Sometimes the husbands remind her of Raymond—their hair rumpled the way his becomes when she runs her fingers through it, or their strong cheekbones which stand out almost painfully in their faces. Some of them have an air of vulnerability that shows they might yet be blown off course, seduced by another woman. They look as if sometime in their lives they will lie awake in bed staring at the ceiling, torn apart by different impulses, and for this weakness Fiona feels a rush of empathy for these strangers.

Once she saw a woman across the street who looked like Helen. The woman was standing on the porch of a newly renovated house, fumbling in her purse for sunglasses; she wore a white blazer over silk trousers, and her straight, shoulder-length hair separated where it brushed her collar-bone. Fiona stopped and stood for a while, panting, rotating her ankles, watching her from behind a parked car. She waited while the woman crossed the lawn to the sidewalk, her heels tapping neatly, and slid into the passenger seat of a waiting Jaguar. Fiona knelt when the driver glanced in her direction; she pretended to re-tie her shoelaces while he started the car.

Fiona thinks that at any given moment, somewhere in the world, an affair is beginning or ending. Yet she cannot see beyond her own situation with Raymond and Helen. She has fantasized a hundred times about phoning Helen at her office, making her cry out with a few words about her husband's soft kisses on Fiona's face and hands and belly, how he bites her nipples until they are red and sore. She realizes she is obsessed with Helen, who has Raymond's commitment while she does not; she knows he will always return to his wife in the end, no matter who he meets or where he goes. She wishes all the complexity of this devotion could be solidified into a tangible object she could squeeze out of his wife. She wishes this in the hours she spends at the gym, seated on a bench in front of the rack of free weights, watching her biceps curve in hard ridges in the mirror. She thinks of her strong hands around Helen's fine, wifely neck not yet ruined by lines and wrinkles, choking her until she moans and spits up Raymond's love. Then at last she can relinquish her, let her head snap back, her body limp as a doll's that has been played with plenty and can now be retired, passed on to some less fortunate child, or thrown out.

ભ

One day, a year after the beginning of the affair, Fiona shows up at a black-tie dinner to which her lover and his wife have been invited. Fiona has chosen for the occasion a simple white dress with a round collar and lacy cap sleeves. She has thrown up twice today and she feels almost ethereal as she makes her way towards her lover's table near the front of the ballroom.

"Hello, Raymond," she says, extending her hand.

The muscles in his face stiffen in shock. He begins to blink rapidly, as though trying to rid his vision of a speck of dust or a loose eyelash. He touches her hand and releases it so quickly she closes her fingers upon the air.

Helen turns towards her with a polite smile, waiting to be introduced. For Fiona, knowing what the next moment holds makes this one all the more poignant, so that she wants to take a mental picture of his wife this way—her carefully made-up eyes shining, her body expensively dressed and perfumed. Up close she can see the soft sagging skin under his wife's eyes, the faint lines and enlarged pores that no amount of foundation can conceal. She feels a genuine sorrow for Helen, the Helen that is at this moment and can never be duplicated again, the Helen whose world is stable and whose husband, trustworthy. Fiona wants to embrace her there in the sea of tables, among the discreet caterers, in the purity of the moment before she is lost.

The future that may someday open between them

makes Helen's face dazzling in its present painlessness. Fiona takes a deep breath of the air that seems to be visibly flowing and weaving around her. When she opens her mouth she finds she has nothing to say, no words to illustrate the past year of her life. Instead she reaches out, trembling slightly, and strokes the other woman's hair with her fingertips.

Helen pulls away in alarm, stumbling back against her chair as if she has been struck by this stranger whose hand remains suspended in the air. Both women turn then towards the man they love, each expecting him to make things right.

6.

My friend Martin was already in love with someone else when he met Jill, the woman he would eventually marry. Debbie, his first choice, did not love him back. He discovered that she had been cheating on him during the last few months of their relationship—the same months during which he had lain awake at night with her naked face against his chest and thought, *I want to have children with this woman.*

He called me soon after they broke up, and we met for dinner in a restaurant downtown. It had been at least six months since I had seen Martin; he had been busy establishing himself at his father's broker- age firm. I thought my friend looked terrific—not for him the wan, suffering countenance of one who has loved and lost. He had an athlete's broad shoulders, an intellectual's vague, shielded eyes, and a lock of hair that sprang over his forehead no matter how frequently he pushed it back.

"You know what I want most, Fiona?" he said, jabbing at his tuna carpaccio. "I want to sleep with her one more time. I have it all planned out. I'd tell her I forgive her, I'd tell her how much I missed her, and then I'd get her into the bedroom and fuck her. Then, right after she comes—*right* after—I'd snatch her clothes up from the floor and throw them in her face. Hah! 'Get dressed, you pathetic slut! I want you outta here!' She'd still be a quivering wreck on the bed, and I'd turn on my heel and leave her. See how she likes it, for a change."

"Hmm. Well," I said, "are you seeing anyone now?"

"There is someone," he admitted. He looked past my shoulder, at the table of business-suited men by the window. "Jill. She's a lawyer for Legal Aid. She's a really nice person, she's probably the kindest person I know. But she's sort of timid, she doesn't want a lot out of life. I like her, but there's no—well, whatever there was with Deb isn't there with her."

"Maybe she's not the one, then."

He finished his glass of wine, sat back in his chair. A passing waitress smiled at him, and he watched her retreating figure, so curvacious it was almost comical, with a meditative frown. "I guess that depends whether or not true passion is important, right?"

೭ఎ

It wasn't long after that dinner that I met you and felt, myself, for the first time in love. You tried not to talk about your wife, but I knew that I came a distant third after your work and Helen. We had terrible fights in which I would say one wounding thing after another, until you drew in your breath and walked out the door. You were, above all, a pragmatic man who could calculate if a property was worth the risk it took to obtain it. In the end you must have decided I wasn't, because you went back to your wife who never knew you had been missing in the first place.

After you left, I called one of my girlfriends in desperation and told her about you. I didn't feel close enough to any of my friends to go into detail about the relationship, but Sharon was sympathetic to what little I said; she described an affair of her own that had somehow lasted for five years.

"We would have these fights, and I would yell at him and cry, and be horrified afterwards because here I was—this smart, independent woman with a great career—and I'd open my mouth and these clichés would come pouring out. It was like I didn't have control over myself anymore. I finally figured out I had to end it one weekend when his wife was out of town. I was staying over at his house; I'd had a lot to drink, and in the middle of the night I crept downstairs to the bathroom and curled up into a little ball under the sink and just cried and cried. I stayed there all night crying while he slept upstairs, and then finally in the morning I unlocked the door and left."

Sharon was the most composed person I knew, and I had a hard time picturing her, in her wire-rimmed glasses and Donna Karan blazers, as a tearful mistress.

"Anyway, about your fellow. He's married," she reasoned. "He was always married. So the fact that he left you doesn't qualify as a Class A rejection."

Despite her attempt at commiseration, I was still destroyed. During the next few months I felt like I was living under a waterfall; I ate and slept and worked as usual, but it all seemed to take place in the distance, drowned out by what had happened with you.

So I was glad when an invitation came to one of Martin's dinner parties, which he held twice a year in his apartment downtown. They were always attended by the same dozen or so people—mostly young doctors and lawyers in suits and ties, and several local artists, actors and writers.

Jill, Martin's new girlfriend, turned out to be a lovely but skittish woman who rushed at me with a tray of drinks as soon as I walked in the door. She wore her brown hair loose around her shoulders, and spent the evening constantly rearranging it, smoothing strands of it down like it was a pet or a fur collar. I would have liked her better if she hadn't made me so nervous. Her anxiety was infectious, her desperate desire for the party to be a success meant that she watched her guests in an agony of apprehension—after all, at any moment one of them might do something socially painful, like begin to stutter, or burst into sobs. I began to be afraid that I would inadvertently do something to make her feel sorry for me, thus ruining her evening. During cocktails, while we were seated around the living room, I attempted to engage her in conversation by mentioning a play I had recently seen.

"Oh, I hardly ever go to plays," she said apologetically. "I just get too nervous, watching the actors. Martin always gets wonderful seats for us, but I sit on the edge of my chair and I can't relax. I'm just sure they're going to mess up their lines, and I end up missing the whole play."

The dinner was spectacular as always. But I could not stop thinking about you. As course after course was brought to the candlelit table I felt as if I was watching a film being run through a scratched, blurry projector. The faces were blurred, the dialogue slow. I had the curious feeling that I could predict what would happen next; there was something achingly familiar about this dinner. Then I realized that so much time passed between Martin's dinners that we would forget the conversations we had had six months ago and would ask the same questions of each other and relate the same anecdotes. Listening to the conversations around the table, I knew I had heard them all before. There was the young East Indian doctor who marvelled about how he did not get sick even though when he went to visit his family back home it was monsoon season and he had stupidly bought a quart of watered-down milk from an old woman in the market. There was the young wife whose husband had over the past year become the country's leading medical link between the AIDS community and the media; she complained at length about her husband being recognized in restaurants and at the opera, and how sometimes they received hate mail and threatening phone calls, but the disgust in her voice never quite managed to conceal her awe at these exciting changes in their lives. And then there was Monique, the model; the bane of her life was that she was considered too pretty for high-fashion work. "I'm just not ugly enough, I don't have some weird flaw in my face that would make it stick out," she would say. She wore low-cut gowns in which her breasts somersaulted freely, and she ate nothing but the garnishes on her plate, sucking her fingers afterwards in a parody of greed, keeping her eyes trained on the men around her as she released each finger with an audible slurping sound. At every other party she would have too much to drink, and then she would tell the story of how once she got so excited in the middle of foreplay that she peed the bed, and how this had not deterred her boyfriend—they had turned the mattress over and continued. At the next party she would remember what had happened at the previous one, put her hand palm down over her wineglass, and restrict herself to describing the silver-haired president of her modelling agency—"the sexiest, the handsomest older man I've ever seen; oh my God, I don't know what I would *do* if he asked to sleep with me."

This was one of her sober evenings, so after dinner I went looking for Martin who was in the kitchen, putting on coffee. "Big success, as always," I said, reaching up to kiss his cheek.

"Thanks. Stay here a while, talk to me. Did you get a chance to chat with Jill?"

"For a little while. So," I said, drawing up a stool from the counter, expecting disclosures, "how are things *really* going with her?" I experienced the guilty thrill people get from talking about someone behind their back, particularly someone to whom we have just been pleasant, even admiring. As a teenager I had often committed minor, and sometimes major, acts of betrayal. They were never planned, and seemed to rise out of a sudden access to a well of meanness inside myself that I was usually unaware of the rest of the time. My most vivid memory of this was something that happened after a fight with my mother when I was fifteen. I had been caught skipping class and she had immediately, and wrongly, presumed I had spent the afternoon with a boy. She chased me around the house calling me a slut and a whore, spitting with contempt. Afterwards I went to stay for a week with the parents of a girlfriend who was studying in Europe. Her father was a bookstore owner, her mother a housewife who had the open, guileless face of a farmgirl. They were in the process of separating, and the night before I went back home Mrs. Morrison and I sat in front of the fireplace and shared a bottle of wine. She was wearing a long paisley dress and I remember how she held her wineglass like a cup of tea, her hands wrapped around it as though for warmth; her fingernails were bitten down to ragged crescents.

"We've had a good marriage," she kept saying. "I

shouldn't be telling you this, but I can't stop wondering who he's going to sleep with first, after we split up. Maybe he's already seeing someone, I don't know, I can't bring myself to ask him. I feel crazy with this. At least every night that he's still here I'll know he isn't in another woman's bed."

Later that night he came to my room, bumping against an old rocking chair, a recent shipment of books. "Take off your T-shirt," he whispered. His glasses glinted in the dark. Suddenly I wanted to make his wife suffer, as though she were my mother. It was over quickly, and afterwards I went to the kitchen for something to drink. I was intensely thirsty, and drank straight from the opened carton of orange juice in the fridge. When I turned around I realized how unfamiliar their house was at night; I groped for a light switch but ended up having to negotiate the stairs in the dark. At the top, I was confronted by two closed doors—I could not remember which was the guest room, and which was his wife's bedroom. After a moment I clenched my teeth and chose, opening the door to my right, and there she was, rising from the bed in her nightgown, the female shape of her with her hair spilling like wax down her shoulders, her voice soft—"Ian? Is that you?"—and I said, "No, no, it's me, I've got the wrong room," and she said, gently as a mother, "Oh. That's all right." She murmured sleepily, settling back under the comforter. "Night night."

Mr. Morrison had already returned to his study, where he had set up a cot. He left for work early the next morning, avoiding a potential scene. It scared me for a while, how easy it was to hug his wife and thank her for her hospitality, promising to work things out with my own family, before going back home.

"So what's the real story with Jill?" I said now, to my friend. "She doesn't seem like your type. Are you still pining after your lost love?"

Martin turned around from the cupboards where he had been taking down cups and saucers. He gave me a grim, warning look. "Things are going great with Jill."

I sensed I had been rude, but in my embarrassment I couldn't help myself, I kept going. "Oh come on, you can tell me. Everyone's out there listening to Monique tell her silver-fox story; she's got half the guys wishing their hair would turn grey so they could ask her out."

"Jill and I are very happy together," he said tightly, staring at me, defying me to contradict him.

I was the first to look away. "I'm sorry. This sounds serious."

"It is." He paused, turning a cup around in his hands as though inspecting it for cleanliness. "We're planning to get married—so shut up, all right?"

I left early that evening; Jill's arm crept hesitantly around my waist after she handed me my coat. "I'm so glad to meet Martin's friends, at last," she said.

"Thank you for dinner," I said. Martin was standing behind her, his hands on her upper arms. He watched me expressionlessly as she twined her fingers through his and brought one of his hands to the side of her face. She flushed, and I could see by the sudden dizziness of her eyes that she was in love.

❧

Martin and Jill got married and bought a house together, with their parents' assistance. I spoke to him on the phone once in a while; he had been made a partner in the firm, Jill was pregnant and they were having a terrific time furnishing the house. Our conversations were brief and always positive.

Just before Christmas, Martin called and said he was having a party at his house.

"And I'm a father now," he said. "As of three weeks ago. It's a boy!"

It was dark when the taxi pulled up their driveway. I walked up to the front door, but before I could grasp the knocker Martin yanked the door open. "Hey, Fiona!" We hugged; he had gotten heavier, and wore his shirt tucked loosely into his trousers.

Then Jill came up the hallway, holding the baby in her arms, her face bent over the child. She was wearing long, drifting layers of silk, like an Indian woman in her sari; there was a tranquillity to her movements that made her seem like another person. If she hadn't reached up to pat her hair before smiling at me, I might not immediately have recognized her.

"This is little Andrew," she said.

I bent over the bundle in her arms. The face that turned up at me yawned and puckered. The skin over the baby's fists was nearly translucent, the blue veins showing through, the fingers like a bunch of raw shrimp.

93

"Feel this," she said, "the centre of his head is still soft." She passed her hand over the curve of his skull, which was feathered with hair. I did the same, but it felt solid to me.

"No, right here. You can press harder than that, you won't hurt him."

I put my fingers where hers had been an instant before and then I found it, the indentation, like a bruise, of where he was most vulnerable, the bones not yet completely grown over the brain. A pulse of feeling coursed through me, beyond sense and possibility—for a moment, I wished I had become pregnant with Raymond's baby.

Martin took my elbow and gave me a quick tour of the house. It had half a dozen bathrooms and bedrooms, a huge kitchen, hallways lined with floor-to-ceiling windows through which you could see across the backyard to another wing of the house. Many of their guests were gathered in the living room; only a few belonged to the group who used to attend his dinner parties. This new crowd consisted mainly of married couples who talked in low, polite tones; several of the young wives had brought their babies, and bags of diapers and blankets. They wore comfortable shoes and no makeup, and their faces were preoccupied and happy. Monique was there, posing by the stereo system, but the glances the men gave were absent-minded and faintly puzzled, as if they weren't sure how they were supposed to react to her.

A few hours later I found myself out on the deck with Martin, overlooking the empty blue shape of the pool. Nearly all his guests had left, gathering their heavy coats and strollers, accepting the foil-wrapped remains of the desserts and appetizers Jill had made for the party. Martin took a meditative sip from a can of diet pop as he leaned back against the wooden railing, looking out at the shadows and light that were his property.

"Did you happen to talk to Allan's date?" he asked after a while.

Allan, a young lawyer, had been one of his dinner party guests, though we'd never exchanged more than a few words. He had shown up briefly that evening with a woman on his arm; she had feathered blond hair and wore a black Lycra dress. They had left shortly after; it was Saturday night, and his date didn't look like she would be happy spending it drinking mineral water and talking to women as they breast-fed their children.

"No, not really, she didn't seem the talkative type."

"I mean, did she say two words to anyone? Did she even have a name?"

"I think it was Tiffany."

He laughed derisively, a sharp explosive sound in the night air. "Allan—he does well for himself, I'll say that. But boy, he's going to discover it stops being enough real fast."

"I love your house," I said, trying not to sound jealous. "Jill looks wonderful, and I can't believe you're actually a father. Are you happy? I mean, is everything as you thought it was going to be?"

He looked past me towards the kitchen, which shone through the wall of windows. We could both hear Jill calling him, faintly, then louder, and then she stood in the doorway with the baby still nestled in her arms, and a man and woman behind her.

"Honey, the Curtises are leaving," she said. "I thought you might want to come with me to see them out."

Martin crumpled the can of soda in his hand, and turned to me with a smile. "Yes, I am," he said. His eyes gleamed, I thought with pleasure. "Getting married, having kids—it's incredible when you find the right person. It isn't like anything you've ever known before."

I watched him walk across the deck, towards his family, his extravagantly lit house. I was thinking of the time you had used those same words to describe your marriage; it was at the beginning of our affair. I remembered that, in the end, it was your marriage that had lasted, it was your marriage you had returned to—and then I followed my friend into the house where, in the living room, someone had finally put on some music.

7.

Fiona was watching a man across the room who reminded her of Raymond. He had grey hair and wore a black suit; the shoulders of his jacket were sharp as if they had been drawn with a triangle and the point of a new pencil.

The fund-raiser for the arts community was being held in a hotel ballroom downtown. It had a high transparent ceiling crossed with white beams; it was like being in a glass cave. Fashionably, the men wore whimsical cartoon ties; the women were outfitted in black dresses and retro shoes. A gallery owner Fiona disliked had turned up in an off-the-shoulder gown made of some shiny, heavy fabric; feathers sprouted from her hat and her opera-length gloves. She looked a little like an emu and kept intruding into the periphery of Fiona's vision.

Fiona kissed the cheek of a photographer she had not seen for several months; the woman had become pregnant, and all evening kept one hand cupped against her belly. A young gay sculptor had pierced the corner of his mouth since Fiona had seen him two years ago, and a half-ring like a horn protruded there, a sliver of gold against his cheek.

"How are you?" she said, "how have you been?"

"Great," he said. "You look fabulous."

"You look great too," she said. "I can't believe it's been two years."

"Two years," he marvelled. "A lot of bodies."

She laughed. "It used to be like that for me, too."

"But I'm single now," he said. "Again."

The man Fiona was watching had moved so that now he stood against a slab of rock that had a white silk flower stuck in one of its cracks. An artificial waterfall glittered next to him, water pouring down into a trough with spouts and drains at the bottom. Fiona excused herself and headed in his direction, nodding to people she recognized along the way.

Up close his resemblance to Raymond was even more pronounced—the prominent cheekbones, the taut, pale skin, his gaze which when he turned it upon her was cautious and in some basic way disinterested. It made her want to prove that she had no intention of injuring him, yet that at the same time she was fascinating enough to be worthy of his interest. This was what she had felt with Raymond. "I have only ever felt this safe with one other person," Raymond had said, "and I married her." But it was what was unsafe about Fiona that made her exciting—a pawn, she had sometimes thought, in his brief flirtation with self-destruction. The last time she had seen him, he looked better than he had a year before, when everyone was scrambling to save their businesses in the recession. In his long, loose jacket and slate linen trousers, he looked as if he had stepped off the runway at Calvin Klein. She knew as soon as he walked in the door that it would soon be over—whatever weakness in him that had made their affair possible had been recognized, analyzed and disposed of in executive fashion.

She wondered what kind of love it was that she felt for Raymond when she wanted to see him crippled, when she wanted to break the bones in his wrist or ankle, to smash him so that he would need her again to make him whole.

Fiona introduced herself to the man who looked like Raymond. She had no interest in him; she simply wanted to see his face as he spoke to her, and compare it with the face of the man she loved. When he let his eyes wander over her shoulder, when he leaned back against the rock and twisted slightly in impatience, he looked most like Raymond. But he had a map of lines under his eyes, deep and criss-crossed, which set him apart; they looked as if they had been put there with a razor blade. Just the other day Fiona had noticed in the bathroom mirror that she was developing lines under her own eyes, radiating out from the inner corners, faint but visible. She thought that maybe later she would think back to this time as the year her face began to bear the signs of trouble, the way it would the rest of her life.

They had nothing to say to each other, yet he had unwittingly satisfied her by looking the way he did, by positioning his face so that he resembled Raymond, and thus piercing her with alternating sensations of pain, anxiety and desire. She kept her face impassive, her smile polite and not the least bit inviting or insinuating—he would have no idea that she was involving him in a fantasy.

Soon he excused himself to look for his wife as groups of people started to disband and head for the door, arranging dinner and drinks elsewhere, promising phone calls and invitations. A rather young woman with a bob of brunette hair, wearing a red dress with gold buttons, emerged from a cluster of women nearby. In the meantime other people had come up to say their good-byes to Fiona, so it was through a mingling of faces and bodies that she focussed on the man and his wife leaving the reception. His wife was younger than Raymond's wife Helen by ten or fifteen years, and slimmer, but she had the same light hair. Fiona concentrated on that hair until it was Raymond and Helen who walked out the glass doors into the late, still-bright summer evening. She did not know if it was her imagination, but she thought they were not a happy couple—they did not draw together but remained as far apart as they could walking out the double doors and into the street. It seemed to her that the space between their bodies was wide enough for another whole person to walk between them.

ও

Raymond had been asked to present several of the awards at the arts awards ceremony where Fiona first saw him. She recognized his name from gossip she had heard—he was visible both in the community and the media, yet little was known about his personal life.

"He's been around all these years and no one knows him," she recalled a curator saying. "His wife maybe. And his mistress, if he has one, though I don't know where he'd find the time."

It was something like love when he appeared on the stage and the video monitors. His face was one that was used to being set in expressions of hardness, yet from several rows back she thought she saw the shadows of something vulnerable in the corners of his smile, in the slight weary downturn of his left eye. She recognized someone who was more than he appeared to be, more than he showed to his employees and the media. It was then that she wanted to know him, to protect him. The way she felt this, so suddenly and deeply, was like nothing she had known before.

Two weeks after they had been introduced at the ceremony following his speech, he'd come to town to visit her. He had said, "It was almost instantaneous, what happened when we met. I can't explain it. I was shaking afterwards." She did not tell him about that initial feeling, how she had hardly breathed after he had finished his presentation, staring at the back of his head and the shoulders of his tuxedo jacket, waiting for the cameras to cut away for a shot of him in the front row, his smile, his dutiful applause. She did not tell him it had begun even before he knew she existed.

But a year later when she asked him to leave his wife, tears came to his eyes, and three months after that it was her he left instead. When it was over she was reminded of something a man had said to her five or six years ago. Brian was a designer who lived in a beautiful white-and-chrome house; he was married to a woman who was a pill junkie and always in and out of the psych ward. He had a mistress who lived in another city, and who would sometimes come to visit for weeks at a time. Fiona had not thought of Brian in years, but his name had come up recently at a party, and she had found out that he was still married. No mistress was mentioned. Now she remembered part of a conversation they had had in a fancy Chinese restaurant with red tapestries and marble floors.

"Anyone can be worn down by love," Brian had said.

Was that true? She must have looked skeptical, because he added hastily, "Genuine love, that is. It has to be genuine."

Had she loved Raymond—genuinely? Was there some failure, a lack, on her part? If she had loved him without selfishness, with a pure and virtuous love, would he still have returned to Helen of the sleek chin-length hair and the suits from Holt Renfrew?

Fiona knew that married men rarely leave their wives—especially men whose careers would be damaged in the process, so that the rent, the wound, would spread through their personal and social lives and into their professional lives as well, leaving them no place to retreat from the pain. Fiona had listened to the sobs of girlfriends on Christmas holidays whose lovers were sitting around fireplaces at home drinking brandy with their wives, or tiptoeing downstairs to push presents into their children's stockings. Even while she had made the appropriate noises of sympathy, she had privately thought them stupid to become involved with people so obviously unavailable from the beginning. There was something faintly masochistic about their grief, something repellent about their loneliness. Now she was not so sure that what they had been going through had been their fault. She thought it possible that it was part of something outside themselves, that it was larger than the self, the way love is larger than the bodies and minds of the people it occupies.

❧

If there existed the possibility that Fiona was unworthy of Raymond, that someone else could have loved him in such a way that he would have ended his marriage for her, then what might that worthy person have been like?

In the months after he left her, she began playing a little game at dinner parties and receptions, in shops and malls, between the pages of magazines and in the commercials on TV. The object of the game was to find the sort of woman who would be able to make Raymond leave his wife. Usually it was someone who was professionally good-looking, a fashion model or an actress, someone who had a lot of hair and wore few clothes. Sometimes it was some beautiful, pale adolescent she spotted on the street, a girl in jeans who had stricken eyes and looked like she would die if abandoned. But other times it would be a well-groomed woman in her forties or fifties, highlights scattered through her greying hair, intelligence radiating from her eyes and her cool, mannered smile. In this way Fiona found new wives for Raymond all over the city—women whom she thought possessed the qualities she lacked, qualities that could provoke a divorce. She found herself staring at women during lunch hour on downtown streets, on the terraces of upscale restaurants, in lingerie shops and designer boutiques—staring at them with a detached look on her face while her eyes became urgent and fevered, as though she were a man stalking a woman he did not know, a woman who would fit in the leading role of his dark sexual fantasy.

❦

Fiona had heard of women who allowed their lives to be ruined by men. She had prided herself on being too sensible and self-possessed for that, yet in the months following Raymond's departure she came apart as though some stitches in her had been snipped, as though a thread in her personality had been hooked onto his body, so when he left he pulled that thread and she began to unravel.

One day while shopping in a fitness store she saw on a shelf a pair of runners, white with navy blue soles, that was the woman's version of a pair she had seen him wearing when he came back from the gym; she bought the shoes without trying them on and put them in the bottom of her closet. Another day she went into an antique store and bought a ring she could not afford; the portly woman behind the counter told her it had been someone's engagement ring, and brought out a rectangular mirror which she supported between her palms so Fiona could see the ring sparkle on her finger. She wanted to know the full story behind the diamonds refracting the light in the slim gold band, the story of the person who had brought it into the shop, but the saleswoman could not say.

"I don't like to ask, you understand," she said.

Fiona did understand. Times were hard, she said, tapping her credit card on the counter.

She felt a great need to consume; she bought outfits, low-cut dresses and smart, bright suits, which Raymond would never see but which she felt sure he would have liked. She wore her new clothes to many dinners and parties, eager for compliments, for the knowledge that she might be attractive enough that someone would leave his wife for her. She needed to exhaust herself physically and socially so that when she went to bed at night, she would pull the covers around her and fall instantly asleep, not to wake until morning. Despite her efforts, she often woke in the middle of the night and lay there thinking about him in bed with his wife, wondering if he was awake and turning to the warm body curved beside him, if he was at that very instant caressing her, sliding into her even as she was still partly asleep, if she liked this, if she was pushing her hips back softly against his belly in acknowledgement, in familiarity. Fiona's eyes burned in the dark; she tossed restlessly, thinking of all this.

Once she almost slept with an Italian executive she met at a dinner party; they went back to his hotel room where he ordered up a bottle of fine Italian wine which he made a show of sipping, one arm draped along the back of the couch. When he turned away from her slightly the skin tightened across his cheekbones. In the bedroom he said he adored her body. He put too many fingers inside her; they didn't actually have sex as in the middle of foreplay his lawyers buzzed for him downstairs and he realized he was late for an important meeting. They never resumed that evening as neither had been particularly interested in the other to begin with, and a few days later he went back to his business in Italy, to his ten-month-old daughter and his fourth wife whom he no longer liked to sleep with because she had become depressed and anorexic.

Fiona knew she had hit bottom when one sunny lunch hour she found herself standing, tears running down her cheeks, in front of a Laura Ashley display window featuring a lacy wedding dress the colour of English cream.

The next night she went out for a drink in a bar

with Frank, a colleague at the art college who had just helped his girlfriend move out of his apartment. They ordered beer and ate the smoked almonds in the bowl on the table. Under cover of the music video she told Frank a few things about the affair, keeping back Raymond's name. He congratulated her for her dignity.

"People go crazy over this sort of thing," he said. "Men go home and shoot their wives and kids, women show up drunk at social things and embarrass the hell out of everybody. You haven't been calling him? You haven't tried calling her?"

"No," she said, "no"—she hadn't called Raymond, and she had left Helen alone. She made sure that when she came home at night she was too tired to do anything more than take off her makeup and fall into bed—otherwise she might give in to the whisky in the liquor cabinet, the waiting phone.

"That's great, you're doing fine."

"Maybe I've become one of those women men can have affairs with without fear of repercussion," she said. She was a bit drunk but she felt lighter, the burden of secrecy partly lifted.

Frank laughed. "Uh-uh, I doubt it. Really,

though, what would you have done if he had left his wife, turned up on your doorstep, asked to move in with you?"

Fiona thought about this for a while, even though she already knew the answer, knew it with her whole self.

"I would have tried to make it work," she said.

Fiona walked home that night. The sky looked as if it would snow; the clouds were weighted, full, like a comforter stuffed with feathers. The air was crisp in her lungs, and the sidewalks metallic in the late light. Soon it would be Christmas, then another year. The display in the Laura Ashley window had changed, of course—now the headless mannequin wore a long corduroy skirt, and a dark velvet blouse with a lace collar. The wedding dress had gone. Whoever had walked into the shop, tried it on and paid for it, was by now settled in her new life.

8.

When I first met you I thought your eyes were blue. The room was crowded and outside the rain hurtled down into the street, loud as a war, almost as loud as the reception. There were women in flickering dresses, men in tuxedos, wine and cigarette ash spilling onto the concrete floors. You stood there with your steady eyes and your mouth a motion away from mine, and I felt the shift inside me. Was it possible to recognize the beginning of one's own life, twenty-four years into it? It seemed fitting you should have blue eyes, like a fairy tale prince.

It didn't matter that your eyes were in fact grey, or that you were married. Something happened as soon as I looked at you, something I could not take back or ignore. It was a recognition, a certainty such as I had never felt before. It was like looking into a mirror: the keenness of your gaze; your quick, concealing smile meant to convey an openness you were guarded against; your passionate gestures. And something else—the hint of some fear or weakness, traces of something that had happened to you a long time ago and had dictated the shape of your life.

 co

It was a windy spring afternoon, two days after we'd met, and the streets were full of pollen. The traffic lights swung hard above the intersection, and passersby pushed their way down the sidewalk with their collars and coats flapping around their bodies. The only spots of colour were the newspaper boxes on the street corners, yellow and red, like the interiors of fast food restaurants.

You were halfway through the revolving doors of the hotel when I rolled down the window of the taxi and called your name. You turned swiftly, as though frightened by something, and looked at me the way one looks at an enemy. When you saw who it was you relaxed a little, though not too much—you couldn't be sure yet that I wasn't an enemy. Gesturing for me to follow, you continued through the circling glass doors, unable to stop or turn back.

I did not know that I would see you always as I was seeing you then, caught in the doors like an image pressed into a book, the doors turning and you helplessly turning with them, looking back at me. I paid the driver and got out of the taxi. My legs were trembling as they carried me towards you.

&

In the bar of the hotel the hostess came by to pour a pale chablis into my glass; you asked for a bottle of beer, which you drank slowly and thoughtfully. We were seated by the window, where outside the day was fading. The glass of the beer bottle was clover green; it caught the last flash of light trapped between the downtown buildings, and tipped a green shadow across the tablecloth.

"I change all the time, every day," you were saying. "Nothing in my life stays the same for long."

At that moment I knew that, whatever relationship we might have with each other, I would eventually lose you. All our experiences would merely be markers along the road towards that loss. The nearly physical pain of this, a sharp sensation in my chest, startled me into silence. I barely knew you, how could I already be mourning the loss of you? At the table behind ours a woman in a pink Chanel suit laughed raucously and, distracted, we both looked at her. She had stiff black hair and her purse strap was a chain of gold links. When you turned back you repeated, as though I had not heard, as though you were warning me, "Every day."

When we finished our drinks you drove me back to my hotel. Your car was sleek, black like a pair of sunglasses, and it slid silently through the night. Your fingertips rested lightly on the wheel. I stared out my window, afraid of looking at you too closely, afraid I would give something away. We stopped at the first intersection and you glanced over at me.

"That's not your style," you said abruptly.

"What?"

"That's not your style. That store." You gestured at the storefront across the street; the display window was illuminated by the track lighting inside. There was only one item in the window, a long orange dress suspended on a headless, wire frame body. Next to it was a terra cotta vase, at least four feet high. I had not been eyeing the dress, not thinking about anything except your proximity.

"I wasn't looking at the store."

"Oh." You were quiet for a moment. "I thought that's what you were doing."

We drove on. I tugged at the hem of my black miniskirt. I was so conscious of you it was like the hyper-awareness sometimes brought on by a lack of sleep, or the first stages of drunkenness. We drove past a park where the tenants of a nearby housing project clustered on benches and by the chain-link fence. The trees there were scanty and dark, like paper cut-outs. We drove down a main street where the lights of bookstore cafés and terraced restaurants still glittered. We did not say a word to each other until we were in front of the hotel.

You looked straight ahead, tapping your fingers on the wheel. "I'm coming out your way in about two weeks; there's some business I have to do there. If you want to get together, I'll give you a call when I'm in town."

117

"Sure," I said, and discovered I had been holding my breath. I fumbled first with the lock, which you popped from your side, and then with my seat belt. You watched, making no other move to help me, and then you laid two fingers for a moment against my cheek in farewell. What I felt so overpowered me that I flinched away from you. I had barely reached the sidewalk before you swerved the wheel and the car sped down the street, through a red light.

ɷ

We sat together in the back seat of the taxi as it headed towards the restaurant I had chosen. The blue of the ocean as it flashed past reflected across your sunglasses. It had been a sultry, oppressive day, turning into a mild evening.

The restaurant had distressed walls and ropes of glass that hung from the ceiling, over the window and again over the bar, resembling rain. During dinner, for which I insisted on paying, I could barely taste my food, I was so aware of you. I could have sworn your eyes were blue—an effect perhaps of the track lighting, the tiled floors. The distortion of wine.

Afterwards we went back to your hotel. You

brought us drinks from the minibar, and turned off the lights in the room. Through the high windows the city swam into view; it was where I had always lived, the inspiration for my art, and that night it seemed a place where anything could happen. We sat for hours—you on the floor with your head resting against the seat of your chair, me on another chair by the writing desk where you had scattered some change, your money clip, and your driver's license.

At four in the morning we found ourselves on the bed. You kissed me on the forehead and pulled the covers over our clothed bodies. I took your face in my hands, traced the lines around your mouth and eyes with a fingertip. Your eyelids were delicate, membranous. You lifted my hair and kissed my neck, and pressed my back reassuringly with your palm. I had never felt so protected as when I curled my leg between yours, and rested my face in the hollow of your shoulder. There your skin was warm, the blood pulsing beneath it, and you smelled like no one I had met before. You smelled like something green that had light shining through it—leaves, water in sunlight. I thought I would remember the smell of you and the heat of your body for as long as I lived.

We were awakened simultaneously by the light flooding into the room, and the sound of maids in the hallways. In the bathroom I looked at myself in the mirror—I was pale, my linen dress desperately wrinkled, the mascara around my eyes clotted. During the night the underwire of my bra had dug beneath my breasts, leaving an angry red mark. Yet I was seized by a sort of joy and, aware that you might yet kiss me, I did not bother to put on lipstick.

In the room you were collecting your clothes and papers, shoving empty dry-cleaning bags into the garbage, patting your pockets to check your belongings. When you saw me you sat on the bed and looked at me, silent, watchful.

At the door you came up to me unexpectedly and grabbed the hair at my temples, pulling my face towards yours. The light from the windows behind you was suddenly blinding, pouring across the carpet towards us like a trail of lit gasoline, and I closed my eyes. You kissed me for a long time, so hard my mouth hurt when you released me.

"See you soon," you said.

ℰℛ

A few weeks later I went to another city for a show. You made sure you were there too, scheduling extra meetings so we could have one evening together in your hotel room.

I was uncomfortable when I arrived; I didn't know what to acknowledge about the last time we were together. You, on the other hand, were animated and almost flirtatious—you touched my wrist or my cheek as we talked, you took off your shoes and curled up barefoot beside me on the couch. Once you asked me if I had met anyone—a man—yet.

"Are you kidding? Since we last talked? Of course not."

"Oh, you will. You can't begin to imagine. When you meet that someone, you'll know. There's nothing like it."

I've met you, I wanted to say, but did not. Although it wasn't late, you soon glanced at your watch and said you had arranged for a six a.m. meeting before your plane left the next day.

"Sorry. I have to be on tomorrow, and I need at least a few hours of sleep."

At the door we hugged warmly, the way friends might, and then you kissed me. Your mouth was cold and sweet with the liqueurs we had drunk. You unbuttoned your shirt and drew my face down upon your chest, where your heart was racing. I listened to it as though it were a matter of life and death, as though it were blips on a hospital machine. You reached beneath my sweater and put your hands on my breasts, over the material of my camisole. After a moment you drew back.

"Go on, get out of here," you said.

When I reached for the door handle you dropped to one knee and clasped your arms around my legs.

"No, don't leave," you cried, mockingly. I looked at you and saw that you were laughing at yourself, and at me. I stood there, my purse dangling at my side, not knowing what to do.

You rose and kissed me some more, gently, until our breathing again changed.

"Please go," you whispered against my mouth, genuine and anguished, and instantly I let go of you. I had promised myself I would not hurt you; this seemed the closest to a commitment I could make to us. I stepped out into the hall and you locked the door behind me, the bolt sliding firmly home in the silence. I heard nothing more. Had you gone into the bathroom, were you standing at the counter examining your reflection in the mirror? Were you standing at the windows, looking out onto the stream of taxis in the street, the skyscrapers jungled around you? Or were you still on the other side of the door, holding your breath, hoping I would come back, make some sort of gesture? But perhaps that was a woman's role— to wait, to linger, hoping for a change of heart, the sound of a lover's step on the stair. Probably you had climbed straight into bed and fallen asleep with a sigh.

Yet I stood in the hall for a long time. The carpet was a deep, dusky colour woven with roses, and there was a marble end table and a vase of flowers halfway down the hall. When I went to the elevator I could see in the silver doors my own flushed face, my dark hair disordered. I chewed on my lip. I was distraught and ecstatic, like a young man leaving his date on her doorstep after a clumsy, exhilarating first kiss.

In front of the lobby, I climbed into the first of a line of taxis that was waiting. My hotel was a short distance away. The driver stitched through the banked traffic before escaping down a side street and through an alley. On the block where my hotel stood we passed a corner where a man was waiting, his face stricken in the light from the single working street-lamp on the block. He looked through the window of the taxi and caught my eye. He was drawn to me, like many people are drawn to those who know their destiny in life. The man on the corner followed the taxi to the hotel. I went to my room, then emerged a few minutes later to fetch some ice from the machine. The man was leaning against the peeling wallpaper by the elevator, smoking a cigarette. He wore a hooded nylon jacket; he had a beard and red veins in the whites of his eyes.

"Please," he said. "You don't know me, but I have to talk to you. Let me buy you a drink. Downstairs."

I looked at him calmly, realizing that tonight I wasn't afraid of anything. "Thank you, but no. Goodnight."

"I need to talk to you," he said.

His pupils were the size of pinpricks. I continued down the hall, swinging my ice bucket, aware that my steps were bouncy with the confidence of someone so deeply involved in her own world that she knows she cannot be hurt by anything from the outside.

"Sorry," I said, turning finally. "I've already had a drink." I paused, and then I grinned. "With someone. I'm seeing someone. A man."

The words felt awkward in my mouth, and amazing.

"Oh," the stranger said, twisting the butt of his cigarette into the reeking ashtray. He seemed to understand. I thought it was part miracle that he turned then, just like that, pressed the elevator button, and left.

&

You returned again and again to my city, scheduling meetings and conferences here. Each time we met we talked for hours, either in your hotel room or my apartment. You weren't perfect, I discovered—you were narcissistic, quick to anger, sometimes dishonest. Your business dealings had taught you to trust no one, and I felt that in any future relationship with you there would be secrets you would keep from me, ways of hiding yourself from me, a tendency to put distances between us. But we found there was more

that linked us than kept us apart. Gradually, we con-
fessed some of the things that had happened to us,
things about our childhoods we said we had never
told anyone before. I recognized the turbulence
behind your talent, your quick, suspicious mind, your
ability to access emotion like a woman. I came to feel
that whatever pain and conflict might accompany our
relationship, whatever deceit or eventual betrayal, it
would be worthwhile.

We seldom went out which, to my surprise,
appealed to me. I did not want to share you with the
world. Increasingly, when you were not there, I found
I did not feel entirely alive. My work, which had been
the centre of my life until now, ceased to absorb me. I
would find myself in the middle of the day in my studio, unable to concentrate on the images in front of
me because I would be thinking about you. You had
once told me how much you admired my ability to
focus on my projects, how even though we were in
different professions I reminded you of yourself at the
start of your career. I felt now that I was losing my
focus—or, rather, that it had shifted so it was on you
rather than on my work.

We still had not had sex, and we never spent the entire night together again.

༄

One evening when you were in town, I went to see you at your usual hotel. You came to the door barefoot and wearing an old company T-shirt and jeans you had hastily pulled on. You poured us both drinks from the minibar, then another, and another. Several times I caught you looking, a wistful expression on your face, at the bare place on my thigh where my skirt revealed the top of my stocking. At two o'clock in the morning, we fell into silence. I took a breath and got up from my chair. You had put your feet on the coffee table, and I knelt and touched your ankle, my fingers trembling. When I glanced up, you were looking at me with an expression of gravity and pain.

"Come here," you said.

We kissed, your hands sliding up my sleeves. I could hardly bear what I was feeling—the relief, the excitement, and something that was like a foretaste of sadness. It was with this edge of grief that I unfastened your jeans. You were naked underneath. I took you in my mouth. I had never wanted to do this before with anyone, had done it in the past only under force or coercion. Now I sensed that this motion was a step forward towards something, a beginning or an ending. I knew which it was. Suddenly I wanted to cry, but already you were touching my shoulder, moving away.

"No," you said. "We can't do this."

You rose, staggering slightly, and brought us two bottles of water from the minibar. Moonlight was pouring in from the window, like an insult.

"It's late," you said. You shook your head. "You've got to go. We'll talk about this tomorrow, I've got an hour or two between meetings in the afternoon. Are you okay?"

"I'm sad," I said. To my surprise, a tear ran down my cheek, and I brushed it away with the back of my hand before you could see. My mouth was still warm with you, and being pried from you felt like a part of myself had been severed.

"You shouldn't let me hurt you," you said.

&

"You can't stay long," you said when I showed up at your door the next afternoon. "Do you want a drink?"

"If you'll join me." I couldn't bear to look at you. In daylight the mahogany surfaces of the hotel room shone, and everything had corners. Your suits hung in the open wardrobe, and your Powerbook was propped open on your desk. It was hard to imagine darkness and our clumsy passion.

"I wanted you, last night," you said. Our fingers touched when you handed me the miniature liquor bottle. "I made a fool of myself."

"No!" I exclaimed. "You didn't. You weren't a fool; I wanted you too." I sat back suddenly in my chair, overcome by the force of my emotions. I had not known until now what it was like to want to reach out to someone so badly I felt myself pulled physically towards him. I felt myself turned almost inside out with my desire to be with you, to take on any pain and confusion you might feel.

"I've never done anything like this before," I continued. "I care about you. I've never felt like this before."

"I have," you said so bluntly that I looked up, startled. "Look, this isn't the first time something like this has happened. I'm not a good person, I've had affairs before, I've cheated on my wife. But that was a long time ago. I do love my wife. Do you believe me? I really love her. I can't have an affair with you."

"Then I guess that's it," I said numbly.

"We'll be friends!" you said. You leaned forward, clasping your hands between your knees. Earnest, pleading. "The other thing—it wouldn't last. But we can be friends."

⁊

I have a friend named Darren who lives in the same city as you. Over the past year I had inadvertently mentioned to Darren, on one of our occasional long-distance Sunday evening conversations, that I had finally met a man and that he was married. When I told him your wife's name—Helen and Darren are both in publishing—he knew who I had been seeing.

A few weeks after you went home again, Darren called. We talked for a while, and then he said, "By the way, I was out last weekend and I saw your pal and his wife. Hmm. That was interesting."

I choked. "Oh God."

"No, it was no big deal. It was a nice afternoon, so I walked down the street and had a cappuccino on the terrace of this café in my neighbourhood. Raymond

130

and Helen were sitting out there eating lunch. I recognized her right away—we've attended a lot of the same book launches and receptions over the years."

"Oh, I can't believe this." My head had begun to pound. "You have to tell me what happened!"

"Nothing happened," he said. "They were just there. I said hello to Helen, we shook hands, we talked a bit about people we know professionally. You know. Not a big deal."

"Do you think she's beautiful?"

"No, she isn't beautiful. At least I don't think so. She's just—average. She isn't tall, she isn't short, she certainly isn't thin. But I wouldn't say she's fat, either. She's just ordinary. Why is this interesting?" he asked rhetorically.

"What about him?" I said.

"Who? Oh, you mean her husband. *Mr. Right,*" he said sarcastically. "I really don't understand this thing you have for him, Fiona. He's just this hotshot business guy, there's nothing to him, I don't know what you two have in common. I don't think he's the sort of person who thinks about anybody but himself. I know, I know, he's your prince. Jesus. One day you're going to look back and you won't know how

131

you could have fallen for such a jerk. You don't believe me, of course."

The questions I wanted to ask my friend, I knew he would not—could not—answer. I wanted to know what kind of a day it had been, if Helen's heels had sounded when she crossed the patio, if husband and wife had been sitting side by side or across the table from each other.

What would you have been wearing, drinking coffee with your wife on a weekend afternoon? Charcoal slacks you would normally have worn with a suit on a weekday? Had it been warm enough for shorts? Could you have been wearing the same pair of blue jeans you had worn that night in the hotel room when I had reached for you and taken you into my mouth?

ひ

The next time you came to see me, it was at my apartment. I reached up to kiss you on the lips, which startled you, but you kissed me back. "I've been doing a lot of thinking," you said.

In my living room you were restless and could not seem to find a chair in which you could get comfortable. You moved from sofa to loveseat to armchair, and finally settled for a space on the floor near the hallway.

"It would be easier for me to say this if you were here," you said, patting the floor next to you.

We sat side by side, holding hands, like children. The sun was setting in the city, and I could see bits of the red sky reflected in the face of my television. The walls of my apartment, bright white at noon, were now grey as rags.

"I've thought of leaving my wife," you said.

I held my breath. I was afraid to move, to jeopardize the moment. It occurred to me that this was how someone who was holding a lottery ticket, who had matched every number so far and was waiting for the last to be called, might feel.

"I was fantasizing about running off with you. I began to question all the choices I had made in my marriage, and in my life."

I could hear your watch in the silence. It was expensive and didn't tick; instead it had a slurred, rushing sound, a bit like water running over stone.

"I don't know if you want to hear this."

"Tell me. I'm ready." I let out my breath. The ball

had dropped, and I knew I hadn't won—I didn't need to hear the announcer call out the number.

"Well, you see, you had a role in what I decided. If I hadn't met you I would have gone on without thinking too much about my marriage to Helen. But for the first time I was forced to look at what I had. And I came to a decision. I will stick by it, too, no matter what happens between us, or whatever happens in the future. I'm not leaving her, Fiona. Not ever. You know the cliché? The vow? 'Till death do us part'? Well, it's true. I made a promise to this woman. It would kill me to go back on my word."

I felt like you had shoved your hands between my breasts, into my rib cage, and were slowly ripping me open. It was unbearable to me that my presence in your life had cemented your vows to your wife, rather than torn them apart. What I had dared to hope was lost; it had never been anything more than my fantasy.

"I'm glad you told me," I said, struggling to keep my voice steady.

"Are you?" Your voice was thick. "I feel safe with you. There's only one other woman I feel safe with, and I married her. Fiona, put your arms around me," you said. You unbuttoned my shirt and touched my breasts, unaware of my pain. I felt frantic, panicked, like someone about to be left at the side of a deserted road. I tore at your pants and you had to help me pull them down your thighs; my hands were shaking, you thought mistakenly with sexual passion. This time you let me suck your penis, but when I made a motion to pull up my skirt and sit astride you, you pushed me away.

"No, we can't do that, I told you," you said.

"What do you think we've been doing?" I said. My voice was high and thin, strange to my own ears. "For nearly a year. What have we been to each other?"

"I thought we were friends," you said. You belted your pants, and rose to stand against the wall. The apartment had grown as dark as old canvas. "I care about you. I would do anything for you."

"But not leave her," I mumbled.

"What?" You took my face in your hands, ran your thumbs over my eyelids, down my cheeks, across my mouth. "Fiona, Fiona. Baby. Oh baby, baby, baby." You took me in your arms and stroked my hair, but I was like a child who would not be comforted. I struggled. "Fiona, listen to me. What good would I be to you if I left her? I'd be as good as dead. I wouldn't be able to do anything for you then."

"Do you think I want you to do anything for me?" I cried. "I don't want anything from you! I want you!"

"You know you can call me if you ever need anything," you said, as though you hadn't heard. "If you needed help with anything, I'd give it to you."

"You don't understand," I said. "You don't know what I'm feeling at all. I wish you would go to hell. Just fuck off and leave me alone."

You were silent for so long, your face turned away, that I caught my breath, afraid. I tugged at your sleeve.

"Oh, I'm sorry," I said. "I didn't mean that. You're angry at me now."

"No, I'm not." But you pulled your arm away, and went over to the chair where you had left your jacket. "I have a plane to catch tomorrow morning. I have to go."

"You're always leaving me," I said. I slid down the wall to the floor. One of my stockings had begun to run, and I picked at it with my fingernail. The room was so shady that I felt I was slipping into another world, away from reality. It was a world of pain, in which I was being abandoned, in which I was losing control. Everything I had built for myself over the years melted away, and all that remained was a wilderness of childhood incidents, and of memory.

"I'm not leaving you. You have my number at work, you know how to reach me."

"Yes, you're leaving. I'm not going to let you go. I can't just watch you leave me." Still I did not move from my position on the floor.

"Look, I don't know what's going on," you said. "I don't understand everything that's happened to you in the past. You've told me some stuff and I guess maybe that's why whatever's going on right now is happening. But I'm not responsible for you hurting yourself like this. Please call me a cab."

"I won't."

"I'm not kidding, Fiona, come on."

"No."

"Well, fuck!" You turned on your heel and started down the hall. "I'll just go to the corner pay phone and call one myself then!"

"All right, all right, wait." I went to the phone

and pressed a button, and gave the taxi company my address. You watched me from the hall, suspiciously, until I hung up and faced you. It was then that I realized you had removed my shirt sometime during our aborted lovemaking, and my awareness of my half-nakedness in contrast to your zipped linen jacket made me feel powerless and angry again.

"Please don't leave me," I repeated. It was too dark in the hall for me to see the face of the man I was speaking to; it might have been my father.

"I'm not leaving you."

"If you walk out that door, you will break my heart," I said.

You sighed and walked out the door. A few minutes later there was the sound of the taxi in the street.

❧

For the next month I did not hear from you. Like the infatuated adolescent I had never been, I waited by the phone and was rude to my friends and colleagues, my voice sharp with disappointment, when they called.

On quiet days I found excuses to walk past the hotel where you stayed, the restaurant where we had eaten. When I did, I would glance surreptitiously at

138

these places like someone passing the scene of an accident in which all the gory details are exposed—the splash of blood on the tar road, the limb with its tattered blue cuff, glass piercing the vulnerable forehead. I felt a terrible compulsion to return to the rooms where we had embraced, but I knew that if I did I would be crossing some invisible line into territory from which I could not return. I thought I could understand now how some women went crazy with grief and murdered the husbands or lovers who had left them. The feelings I had had with you were not ones I could duplicate elsewhere. These feelings were somehow exclusive to you, and to lose you was to lose all prospect of experiencing again such vitality and happiness.

I spent as few evenings alone in my apartment as possible. I accepted invitations to art gallery openings and cocktail parties where I was accosted for conversation by would-be artists, many of them eager, anxious middle-class women with damp locks of hair over their foreheads. They were in their early forties, like Helen, and I found myself scrutinizing their faces and rejoicing at the lines around their eyes and mouths, the inelastic muddiness of their skin. In these surroundings I felt almost comfortable, and I thought it was because I could be certain everyone around me was unfulfilled in some way. There were the society wives in their Louis Feraud suits and inherited jewellery, the enigmatic husbands holding drinks in their hands and nodding courteously. I listened half-heartedly to the meaningless voices around me, shook hands with people whose names I promptly forgot, felt like I had drunk too much even when I did not drink at all, and only went home when I was so tired I thought I might sleep.

Other nights I went out with friends my own age—lawyers, teachers and doctors who, in their mid-twenties, were just at the beginning of their careers. They gave garden parties in the backyards of their rented houses, and went to trendy restaurants with *trompe l'oeil* murals and waiters who dashed wine-glasses onto the terra cotta floors. Sometimes we went to nightclubs where the walls were painted the bright colours of candies, and young women my age giggled, flirted and ordered drinks made with melon liqueur and grenadine. The girls wore Doc Martens and filmy slip-dresses; the boys had textured platinum hair and tried to distinguish themselves with piercings through their eyebrows. After too many cocktails I would try to tell my friends about you, but I had the impression they thought there was something wrong with me. Whenever I began to describe my obsession for a man in his forties who was married and lived in another city, they would try to change the subject, or fall into an embarrassed silence and pretend to be absorbed in stirring their drinks. I felt that none of them had had their lives turned inside out by another person; they had yet to be defined by any real emotional experience, and I felt increasingly detached from them. I missed you even more in these places, knowing you would not belong, and I went home dizzy and sometimes nauseated. When I looked in the mirror above the sink I saw a face that with each day would loosen its hold on youth. I would never be able to reclaim this part of my life once it was over. And so I went back to the restaurants and clubs, grateful for the moments when the music was so loud or the conversation so boisterous that I did not think of you.

ᚼ

"Guess what?" I said over the phone. "I'll be in town

next week to visit a few galleries and see the new shows. I'll only be there for three days, and I have a lot to do, but are you going to be around then?"

You were silent for a moment, and then there was the sound of pages turning. "Mmm—I want to, but what are the dates again? Shit. I'll be in meetings close to your end of the country. It's not going to work this time—but I'll call you soon, I promise."

When I arrived I discovered I had been put up in a hotel across from the one where you had taken me for our first drink. My days were busy, but in my free time I saw my friend Darren; by mutual, silent consent, we did not talk about you or your wife. On the last evening I met Carrie, a friend from high school, for dinner. We embraced in the lobby and ventured outside, into a brisk wind that had her turning up her collar and hugging her arms.

"I thought we'd go to Prism, the restaurant in that hotel across the street," Carrie said. "It's very *nouveau*, I thought you'd get a kick out of it. I made reservations."

How could I explain that the hotel was off bounds because I had once been in the bar with a man? We crossed the street and, in order to reach the main entrance with its revolving doors, walked past the bar. There were other couples drinking at their tables by the window, perhaps poised at the beginning of love affairs, or more likely discussing business deals, mutual acquaintances, the day's headlines. I was both dismayed and curiously excited to be returning here without you.

I followed Carrie up the escalator, seeing our reflections in the mirrors above the fountains and indoor gardens. Prism, the restaurant, was a vast expanse of sharp angles, abstract paintings and sleek white surfaces. As soon as we were shown to our seats Carrie ordered a glass of wine, but I asked for a mineral water, afraid that if I began to drink I would start to talk about you.

The food, when it came, was arranged in complex shapes and colours. Several times in the middle of the meal I excused myself to go to the hotel bathroom and splash water on my face. The bathroom was long and marble, like a vault, and every time I emerged to walk back to the restaurant, I expected to see you coming up the escalator. From this angle I would see every part of you—the top of your head in the mirrored ceiling as it slanted with the rising escalator, your shoulders in the mirrored walls on either side of you, the back of your body in the mirror behind you. I almost expected to see you like this, whole and dimensional and rising towards me, and I wondered what I would see on your face—alarm or happiness—but each time there was no one, you weren't even in the city, and I returned to the restaurant with its chrome chairs and glass sculptures. I toyed with my dinner, asked Carrie questions that required long answers so I could merely nod and pretend I was listening, and ordered *tiramisu* for dessert instead of my customary brandy.

When we emerged from the hotel, the wind had become so violent it hurt our faces and scalps. The sky was an icy navy blue, Carrie's coat blew stormily around her body, and the power lines thrummed like whips. "Goodbye, see you soon, come visit," we gasped at each other, and Carrie struggled into a taxi-cab. I fought my way across the street, towards a poster of Drew Barrymore lounging in a Guess ad behind a buckling sheet of plastic on the side of a bus shelter. When I made it to the corner I turned to look down the street to get my bearings, and that was when I saw the store where the orange dress had hung, the dress you thought I coveted that night over a year ago. The dress you thought was on my mind when already I had been thinking of your white skin, my body in your arms instead of inside the expensive curves of fabric. Now the dress was gone, but the window was still lit, and I could clearly see the three wedding dresses that stood behind the glass. They were floor-length, threaded with shining sequins, and the skirts were made of layers upon layers of lace and tulle. The three white dresses hung stiffly in their glass room, away from the wind storm.

ↄ

The days passed and I could not stop thinking about, waiting for, you. It was like some faulty wiring in my brain was causing a single tape of experience to loop around and around; each recollection, each pulse of longing, was as fresh as though it was the first time it had occurred to me.

It was an effort to tear myself away from the phone, the possibility that you might call or visit, but I decided to try to break the pattern of my thoughts

by going away for a week. California. Surely the searing noonday heat, the bruised lavender sky smeared
with haze, the palm trees that looked ready to ignite,
would burn a path of sense into me. I left a message
on my machine saying I was on holiday, and booked a
room in a hotel on the boulevard; the walls were hung
haphazardly with posters of James Dean and Marilyn
Monroe, the carpet was peppered with cigarette
burns, and the plates of all the light switches were
cracked. A sort of lassitude descended upon me, and I
rarely ventured from my room. I found that even the
fragrant air in the canyons could remind me of the
warmth and closeness of your body, and consequently
of your absence. I spent my nights lying awake in bed
listening to tinny strains of opera issuing from the
bedside radio, and traffic reports from the freeways.
Sometimes, out of nowhere, I would be seized by a fit
of anxiety that tightened my scalp and made my
palms sweat—you would not come back, I would live
out the rest of my life without you. I had never before
dreaded being alone the way I did now.

In the mornings I spent long, mesmerized minutes standing naked in front of the mirror tacked

above the bathroom sink, looking at my shoulders, my breasts, my stomach. I wondered what your wife would look like under the same circumstances—better or worse? I knew it did not matter, but I wished I could see Helen like this. I wondered what she smelled like—if she wore designer perfumes, or if a certain part of her body always gave out the scent of apple blossoms, or warm milk, or ginger.

Towards the end of the week, a television host who had featured my work on one of her shows drove up from her home further down the coast to visit me. It had been a few years since we had seen each other, and we almost missed each other in the lobby of the hotel. Teresa was driving a new Mercedes 450 SL, and she had lost ten pounds after turning one of her spare rooms into a gym.

"You look incredible," I said, hugging her. "I love your hair like that."

Teresa held me at arm's length and looked me up and down. "Why, thank you." There was a conspicuous silence, in which she did not return the compliment. "Fiona, you're only here for a little while. Why don't you pack a bag and we'll drive down to my place, and you can stay overnight? I'll bring you back tomorrow. You've never seen my house before."

I agreed, and we drove down a clean grey highway, the Pacific Ocean glittering to one side of us. When we stopped for gas, I watched as my friend went to the pump and then disappeared inside the station. Through the grimy glass I could see her talking to the cashier, throwing her shoulders back and laughing as she pointed at a spot on a map. She had a slight figure, shining honey-blond hair, and from the back she appeared to be a girl wearing the pressed slacks and gold-buttoned and -braided jacket of a well-off woman. I thought that if I were a stranger watching her, I would never have guessed that this was someone who had spent the last five years of her married life in love with another, also married, man.

The beach-front town where Teresa lived was flat and ochre. The downtown streets were crammed with antique shops and tourist restaurants, and driving through I could smell seafood and frying chips. The suburbs were dominated by Taco Bells and Wal-Marts, and communities of multi-levelled houses behind white iron gates and guards in booths like one might see at a border crossing.

Teresa lived in one of these houses with her husband, John. Inside, she shook off her shoes and padded into the kitchen, pouring two glasses of Evian and handing one to me along with a coaster.

"Use this. You're in deluxe surroundings now," she said, somewhat wryly. "You can sleep in the guest room upstairs tonight. Feel free to look around. I'm going to change and use the gym for an hour or so, and then we can see about dinner."

In the fastidiously tidy guest room I tried to turn on the light and mistakenly turned on the ceiling fan instead; each attempt to turn it off merely accelerated the speed of the blades. Giving up, I wandered down the hall into my friend's study. Next door I could hear the silvery clink of weights returning to their place, and soft grunts of exertion. On Teresa's desk, set at a careful angle, there was a photograph of her husband in a leather frame. I picked it up, and my eyes grew moist. John looked remarkably like you—in the photograph his hands were in his pockets and his face was turned to the light. It might have been early evening, the light golden and cold. A lock of hair on his fore-head shone, and his mouth was set.

"That's my husband," Teresa said from the door-way. She was wearing a pink Spandex bodysuit, and had a towel draped around her neck. "I doubt you'll get a chance to meet him tonight. Things are crazy for him at work. Last week there was one night where he didn't get in until three in the morning, and then he was out the door again for a meeting at six. You'll probably be in bed before he comes in."

We went out for dinner that night in one of the downtown restaurants with wood panelling and sky-lights, for plates of steamed artichokes and slabs of raw *ahi*. I asked for a Scotch and Teresa, her cheeks pink with exercise, prudently sipped a single glass of wine. She gave me a look when I ordered another Scotch halfway through the meal. We talked amicably about various Californian celebrities, increasing vio-lence in the cities and suburbs, and a young local author who was getting published in *The New Yorker* and *Harper's*. Several times I wanted to ask her about her marriage, and if she was still seeing her lover, but I did not.

"When I saw you at your hotel, you looked like your best friend just died," Teresa finally said, over our coffees and sorbets. "Do you want to talk about what's going on?"

"You don't want to hear it. It's a man. He's married."

Teresa was still for a moment, her fingers steepled, and then she carefully blotted her lips with her napkin. "You're right, let's not talk about this. If we do, I'll just end up talking about Geoff, and then I'll start crying, and the evening will be ruined. All I can say is, my affair with Geoff has brought me nothing but pain. You know that. And it's the same for every woman friend I have who's ever loved a married man. So what can I say to you? I'm in no position to counsel you. Just be careful."

"I think it's gone beyond that," I said. "And we've never even had sex."

"I loved Geoff for two years before we ever had sex," Teresa said. "That doesn't mean anything. You've seen the picture of my husband. John's an attractive man, he's very dedicated to his work, he's a kind person. So many times I've thought, why am I doing this? But the way I feel when I'm with Geoff—there's been times I've thought I'd rather die than give those feelings up."

"If you'd said that to me a year ago, I wouldn't have known what you were talking about," I said. "I'd have thought you were being melodramatic. Now I understand completely."

She unclasped her purse and reached inside. She took out a tube of lipstick and a compact before unfolding a thin sheet of paper. "This came in the mail from Geoff the other day."

I took the letter and scanned the elegant handwriting. "'I saw you in Santa Monica last weekend. You were on the Ocean Front Walk, alone, you carried what looked like a plastic cup of soda in your hand, you wore dark glasses and the turquoise sweater I love. I could not take my eyes off you. It was like being under a spell. For the next hour I drove and parked, drove and parked, parallel to you, just so I could watch you...'"

I couldn't read any more, I felt like I was spying.

"We'll never have a life together," Teresa said softly, sliding the letter back into her purse. "I'll never leave my husband, and Geoff won't leave his wife.

Believe it or not, we can't hurt those people more than we may already have. Do you understand? I'll never have a life with the man I love."

That night I tossed and turned on the custom-made bed in the guest room. I dreamt that I walked into the bathroom down the hall, the one that Teresa and John shared, and smelled your scent above one of the double sinks. It made me ache with loneliness. It was after nine in the morning when I woke; downstairs, Teresa was talking on the telephone and emptying packets of lite creamers and aspartame into her coffee.

"John's gone to work. He said hi," she mouthed. Then, into the receiver, "Three o'clock? Yes, that's fine. No, it just needs touching up at the roots."

She hung up and wandered into the sunken living room, where I had taken the *Los Angeles Times* and a glass of orange juice. "I can drive you back. We've finished taping the season's shows, so I just have to be downtown at three for a hair appointment."

She stood in the centre of the room for a while, looking at me and then sweeping the walls with her gaze. "Something's wrong. Something's driving me crazy," she said abruptly.

I folded the paper and laid it on the coffee table. I waited.

Teresa shook her head, and then marched across the living room, her heels sharp on the hardwood floor. "It's that painting. It's crooked! Thank God I noticed it. I knew something was wrong."

She settled her fingers on the corners of a painting of a nude woman holding a string of pearls in her lap, tilted it a fraction to the left, then stood back with her hands on her hips.

"That's better. It was driving me crazy. It would have driven me crazy all day. That's a lot better."

She sighed in relief, and then turned and smiled brightly at me. "Ready?"

Back in the city, we parted in front of the hotel with brisk kisses and promises to write. "You take care, now," Teresa called from the car. "Write me about your brilliant career!"

I watched my friend easing her Mercedes out into traffic. The sun gleamed on the car's sleek curves, and on her yellow hair. I thought then that I would trade my career, and all it promised, for a life with you. But I was beginning to understand that the sheer force of my will was no longer enough to make things happen. I could want someone with all the strength and emotion inside me, and still I would lose him before he was ever mine.

∾

You did come back one last time, two weeks after my trip to California. You called and invited me to your hotel.

"Hey, it's great to see you!" you said, giving me a hug. You were wearing a black sweatshirt and black Adidas shorts, and you looked bright-eyed, full of energy, like someone just back from vacation. "It's been so long. How are you? Tell me how you are."

"Oh, I'm fine." I settled into the couch. Behind me the sky was deepening, and the lights in the office towers were starting to shine. "I've been producing a lot of work, mainly because I'm only teaching one class this semester. I should have enough for a new show soon. And I spent a week in California, that was fun. Hey," I said, as lightly as I could, "it's really great to see you."

"It's the best." You smiled at me, and bounced into the seat beside me on the sofa. "Before we go on,

I just want to say—let's forget about what happened that night, okay?"

"Okay."

"It never happened."

"It's gone."

"Great. You look so good. Tell me more about your work."

"Well, I—" I was unable to finish my sentence, because suddenly you leaned forward and kissed me on the mouth.

I closed my eyes, I forgot what I had been saying. It seemed to me that I forgot everything I had ever said in my life. Your kiss had been as devastating as an unexpected blow. When I opened my eyes I saw you—your mouth, your cheekbones, your bright, almost reflective irises.

"I couldn't resist," you said, grinning, pleased with yourself. You sat back, watching me.

For the first time in my life, for that instant, I knew I was alive. It had never occurred to me in this way before. Up to that moment, no amount of pain or happiness had made me so sure of my physical existence, and my mortality. At the point of your kiss

I knew in a flash that I was a part of the moving, breathing world around me, that I was solid, involved, inextricably bound up and connected with others. I knew I was not independent, that I needed someone else with whom to discover certain feelings and insights. This was a revelation. And then followed the realization that I would never feel exactly as I did at this moment again, with anyone else, that years later if I was with another man I would think about you, and I would be struck by the immensity of what I had lost.

I leaned over then and kissed you back. Not quickly, not with amusement, the way you had kissed me, but for a long time, like someone saying good-bye—as I knew a part of me was saying, had been saying all along, that there wasn't anything else to be said to a married man but this. This goodbye. Your mouth was like life to me, life that I would give up everything I had to join, because what we would have together would be so much more than I had had before now.

"I couldn't resist," I said. "I am lost. I am all yours."

Then I laughed, as though I were not serious

either, so I wouldn't frighten you. You gave me a quick look, and then you relaxed and laughed too. We talked for a while, and then you kissed me again. Together we unbuttoned my blouse, and you watched as I took off my bra. We went over to the bed where you bit my nipples and I lay down between your thighs, touching you, sucking you. After a while you pulled me up on the bed and held me.

"What do you want from me?" you said. "What can I possibly give you?"

"I want you."

"No. What do you want?"

"You. You."

"You can't have me. I can't give myself to you." You sat up and shook your head. You looked distraught; you ran your hands through your hair, and the lines around your eyes seemed to multiply as I watched. "I keep trying, and I can't. Something stops me. I don't know what it is, but it's there, and I have to listen to it. Here, put your shirt on."

I buttoned it slowly, biting the inside of my lip so I wouldn't cry. You went over to the minibar and got us both a drink, and then sat down on the edge of the bed.

"I missed you so much when you weren't here," I said slowly. "Sometimes I would dream about you. I don't know what to do."

"I think I know now why you behaved the way you did that night." You looked at me. Your face was cold, resolute. In the lamplight, among the still-rumpled sheets, I saw the grey at your temples, the grey of your eyes. "I didn't know before, I didn't think you were feeling this way. You have to look after yourself. I'm not going to be there for you."

I must have flinched in spite of myself, because you reached out then and touched my cheek.

"I'd still like to see you, but not for a while. Maybe in a year or so, we can get together for a drink somewhere and catch up. I'd like to know how you're doing. Maybe we can make it an annual thing, check in on each other once a year."

I was so horrified I could not speak.

"There does seem to be something between us, and I wouldn't want to lose that entirely. I'd like to make sure you keep doing well, but I don't want things to go on the way they have been. I'm not being cold, Fiona, I'm just telling you."

"You're the only person I'll ever want," I said. The words as they formed were a revelation: I had never wanted anyone physically before you. Sex had always been a measure of power or abuse before we met, a way of hurting myself and, sometimes, my mother. "There hasn't been anyone but you, not since we met. I don't think there ever will be."

"No. You're wrong about that. I know what you feel, I've been there. It doesn't last. It'll pass with time."

Then there was something I wanted to say, but could not. I wanted to use the word love, I wanted to tell you that I loved you. You were the home I had been looking for ever since I left my own family, where love was so painful that I had never dared to feel it for another person before meeting you. I had thought for a while I could find another home in my career—in the reviews that lauded my shows, in the increasing acceptance from the artistic community— but all this had not been enough. Since meeting you I felt there was a place for me in the world, a place where I belonged and could be as safe as anyone. I looked at you sitting on the edge of the bed—the slope of your back, the hair curling at the base of your neck, your profile. You were turning your water glass in your hands, and I saw in the light of the bedside lamps the creases around your eyes and the sharply drawn brackets around your mouth. I felt your face had grown as familiar to me as my own.

Although I did not know it then, at least not in a way I acknowledged, I would never see you again. Even if I had known, I could not have done any more than I did that night—which was to hold you as hard as I could in my vision, the way I had always tried to do.

9.

Fiona can only see fragments of people's faces when she walks into the room. Dim, circular lights are set deep into the ceiling, indirectly illuminating an eyelid or a cheekbone, a glinting mass of hair, a gold cufflink. One side of the room is a curve of glass, giving out onto a view of the pier and the ocean, dark blue, the texture of ball gowns.

The faces in the room are not immediately friendly; she had arrived early in the party, when people are reluctant to leave the tight groups they have formed in case they are not easily admitted into others. Fiona accepts a glass of wine from a white-jacketed caterer and wanders through the room, looking for people she recognizes.

"What a wonderful room to have a party in," she says to the elderly couple standing next to her, making conversation. "The view is incredible."

The man and his wife titter politely.

"I think a lot of people will show up later on," she continues. "Do you know many people here?"

The man titters again, covering his mouth with a liver-spotted hand, and the woman leans closer. "What, dear?" Fiona shakes her head and edges away from the couple, pretending to see someone she recognizes across the room. She is saved by the host tapping the side of his wineglass, directing the attention of his guests to where he is standing in front of a row of paintings.

"I'll keep this short, so you can all get on with the party. You might want to thank those people wearing the red ribbons. Otherwise, there's food, there's wine—I hope you all enjoy yourselves. Take your time looking at the terrific local art on the walls around you. Thank you for coming and helping us celebrate the end of another great year."

There is applause, and a man next to Fiona turns

around and vigorously pumps the hand of a woman with a bit of red on her shoulder.

"Thank you," he says. "Was this a difficult event to organize?"

The woman takes back her hand. "Uh, this is a different ribbon," she says, gesturing at her shoulder.

Fiona sees that she is wearing the fashionable red AIDS loop, not the straight bit of ribbon with the rose attached that some other people are wearing. The man is embarrassed and doesn't seem to know how a single compliment, so well meant, could have lead this early in the evening to a social gaffe.

Often when Raymond was in town he was invited to receptions or parties like this one. After a full day of meetings he would give some excuse and show up at her apartment instead. They would sit around in their jeans and socks, kissing and talking, and he would stroke her hair like it was the hair of someone's child he was admiring. That he chose her over the potent mix of social anxiety, boredom and expectation that made these gatherings irresistible, flattered her. But those were the times he was able to see her away from work, away from his wife. He would reach out for her with an oddly detached urgency, as if he were watching himself, as if he were an ex-smoker helplessly watching his own hand close over a package of cigarettes.

It is at parties that she thinks of him most, feels him as a missing limb that tingles still, that occasionally and without warning flares into real pain. She thinks it might be different if she had someone to wink at from across the room the way couples at parties do periodically over the course of an evening, someone she can meet over a tray of cheese or by the bar to touch hands and ask each other, *How are you holding up, are you having a good time, do you want to go soon?*

Sometimes she wants to betray Raymond, and yet she promised all through their relationship that she never would. Each time they were together, when he put his hand on her breast, when he tipped her over onto the bed, his eyes would pluck at her face and with a grim smile fixed to his lips he would say, *Are you going to betray me? Hmm? Are you? Are you?* in a sort of chant, whispering it to her like fierce words of endearment, like dirty words, like pornography, and she would shake her head no and then say, *No, I will never betray you.* She said it with the conviction of someone who believed that what she felt in that instant would never change.

Now she wants to break that promise like it is a wedding vow, and she lets the caterer fill her glass again as she makes her rounds. The room has become so full that she has to wedge herself sideways from group to group. She smiles, she inclines her head attentively, she mimics having a good time. All the while she feels his absence, sees inside herself the rise and fall of his chest, his fingers idly running through her hair or down her back, his face slowly opening and relaxing as she bent between his thighs.

At the awards ceremony where they first met, there were enough people around so that no one heard their conversation, or noticed them moving to a corner of the room. *I think you are someone who would kill to get what you want,* he said to her, a caress in his voice. Other men might try to win a woman by saying, *You are beautiful,* or, *I love you,* but what he said worked on Fiona. She had always been attracted to cruel, ambitious men who sometimes became vulnerable with her and then punished her by leaving.

But then, that was nothing special about her. Lots of women were like that; most of her girlfriends fit that description. One of them, an internationally respected lecturer, had affairs with the men who attended her talks. *Give me an audience of three hundred perfectly decent and friendly men,* she once said, *and I'll pick the one who will do me harm.*

As soon as she met Raymond, Fiona was hooked. The only man she had been with in the year prior to him had been an American executive who visited her once a month when he was in town for business. He was the president of a large corporation and served on numerous boards of directors; he went after money the way other people, her friends for example, went after love. It was almost endearing, his obsession with money—very eighties and passé. Still, it enabled him to bring her amusing presents, and she liked the lack of turmoil in their relationship. He cared so little about the rest of her life that in the year they knew each other he never once asked what she did with her days, if she had any dreams or ambitions. Maybe he thought she did nothing and had none, that when they were apart she took long bubble baths and lounged on a satin-covered couch eating chocolates and talking on the phone to her girlfriends. What difference did it make? After all, she knew nothing about him except that he was married to a middle-aged woman who had lost her figure, that his kids were grown and gone, that he drove himself suicidally at work and considered himself somebody who had never been in love. Whenever she asked what things were like at home, he would say, *Great!*, in an emphatic, falsely cheerful way that discouraged further questioning. Sometimes she fantasized about marrying him and having dual citizenship, and tooling around both countries in his Rolls-Royce while he sat in glass offices talking ungraspable sums of money with other thin-haired men in big suits.

But then Raymond showed up and with him, the loneliness. It had come rolling in, like fog. She woke up one morning to look out and discover that she could see nothing else; everything was obscured by it. That was what he had awakened in her. She had gone home after meeting him and turned in front of her full-length mirror—was this the body of someone who could kill? She felt her arms and legs, searching for hidden, complex muscles.

I am a killer too, he had continued that night, a corner of his mouth lifted as if in mockery. *There are only a few of us in the world, so few that we recognize each other.*

Perhaps Fiona was looking at him with an unbecoming eagerness, perhaps he thought she felt too safe in the exclusive club in which he had just made her a member, because then he lifted one padded shoulder and dropped it and said easily, *Or perhaps I'm wrong, and the world is full of us. I've been wrong before.*

It was then she wanted to clutch his sleeve and say, *No, you're not wrong*, because she wanted to believe she was like him, because he seemed to be one of those rare men who walked enveloped in light, the way beautiful or very stylish women do.

༄

Across the room, a woman Fiona vaguely remembers having met at a Christmas party is waving to her, and she is making her way towards her when she is stopped by hearing Raymond's name.

The sound of it in another person's mouth is

169

incredibly intimate; it wrenches something inside her. She heads toward it blindly, like it is a steady light in a storm.

The man who said his name wears glasses and a pullover, in the rebellious fashion of a man who begrudges the fact that his job requires him to wear a suit and tie. He looks familiar to her, and as she listens to him she realizes he is one of Raymond's former employees; they might have been introduced before, at another reception. He has three lines etched between his eyebrows, like a sparrow's footprint, which relax or deepen depending on his level of concentration, so that they offer a kind of visible barometer of the intensity of his feelings at any given moment. She watches these lines in fascination and extends her glass when the caterer comes around again grasping the neck of the wine bottle by a cloth napkin and pouring generously.

"—and I think he misread the situation," the man is saying. "I think it showed a serious error in judgement on his part, the way he chose to handle things. A lot of people didn't find it so comfortable dealing with him anymore. I could see the discontent everywhere—"

Fiona can't help it, she feels a perverse thrill of enjoyment. She takes a large swallow of wine and leans into the conversation.

"Oh yes, I heard about the situation over there at lunch a few days ago. You must have had a hard time working in that environment."

The man doesn't seem to remember meeting her before, and he is eager for collaboration and support.

"You know about it? I hardly have to tell you, then. He made my last months there a living hell—"

He turns his back on the two men he had been speaking to, and steers her to a corner near the windows overlooking the harbour. The lights have come on all around the pier, and the masts of the moored boats bob against the sky. He touches her arm often for emphasis, and she leans against the glass. It feels cool and soothing against her skin, like Raymond's cheek. She wants to talk about Raymond but she's afraid that as soon as she mentions his name, this man will somehow suddenly know their relationship, that images of her in Raymond's arms will rise in the man's mind, so powerful she feels the breaking of her silence to be. At any moment she could betray him by saying,

I know him, I know his habits, the way he has of looking into his glass before each sip as if checking for poison, the way he coughs and turns on the tap before going to the bathroom, I know what his mouth tastes like and how it feels on my body—but even listening to this man, nodding in encouragement, is a betrayal. She remembers how Raymond had once spoken in scorn of a woman they both knew, who went to meetings wearing provocative outfits that did nothing to flatter her stocky build. *You can't trust her*, he had said. *Give that woman a drink, and she'll say anything.* Now Fiona looks down at her glass and in an abrupt, defiant gesture empties it, as though he is watching. Even when she is drunk, she remains aware of what she is doing. It is like standing on the tracks with one foot stuck between the ties, watching the approach of the train. There is nothing you can do, you can only watch disaster coming. Raymond had that quality too, it showed itself when he touched her, the way he watched his hand reaching out for her with a mixture of dread, desire and an awareness of the pain he would later feel.

"—should exchange phone numbers," the man is

saying, hunching his shoulders towards her. "We can have lunch. It's been great talking to you."

"Are you married?" she asks abruptly.

The man starts, flicking his gaze away, surprised. "Yes."

She nods. She cannot read his intent; the lines between his eyebrows give so little away, after all. The lenses of his glasses appear shaded, but they are only reflecting the darkness of the water and the sky outside. She can't tell if he's interested in her for more than lunch, and she wonders if she can ever drink enough to make herself sleep with him in an effort to get closer to the man she loves. She wonders if she slept with all the men he's worked with, if she could get closer to him. She's even had fantasies of sleeping with his wife, of exploring the same places in her body where he has touched and kissed and convulsed. As if somehow by doing all this she could find him again, trapped at the centre of the cage of other bodies.

∽

Fiona walks a short distance down the hallway to the women's bathroom, outside the room where the party is starting to disperse, men rummaging in their trouser pockets and women in their purses for their coat check tickets.

The bathroom is spacious, enormously mirrored; everywhere she turns she encounters her reflection in quadruplicate—front and back views, and two side views. She feels slightly dizzy, and knows that later in the night she will wake with her heart racing, that she will stumble to the bathroom and in the brilliant light will see again her own fingers writing down her phone number for the man at the party. She had pressed so hard with the pen, thinking of Raymond, that the nib had cut through the creamy stock.

She is sick of herself, sick of what the man in the room who had resumed talking to the two other men in suits must be thinking about her, might eventually find out about her. She wonders if what she is feeling is similiar to what a married woman might feel after making advances to another man at a party, after tentatively agreeing to meet someone over a lunch that turns into a proffered room key, hurried gropings, the shaky re-application of lipstick and the stuffing of soiled panties to the bottom of a purse. The shame, the bitter, exploding taste of betrayal—not only of a loved one, but of the self, of a promise to the self.

Has your wife ever had affairs? she had asked Raymond soon after they first met.

His face was perfectly calm, his voice measured. *If she has, she has been discreet, and consequently I am grateful to her for not embarrassing me.*

But Fiona doesn't have anyone to whom she has promised to remain faithful. She doesn't have the knowledge of a husband's impending grief and disbelief and anger, his head bent in his hands at the breakfast table, his shoulders slumped away from her. Because if Raymond did know about tonight, he would only feel a stab of concern for his career, not for their relationship, which could never be so valuable.

She doesn't even have anyone to betray. This seems to her to be the ultimate injustice. She wants to grab the shining silver faucets, bend over the sink, and sob with her forehead pressed against the tap. But the bathroom, with its floral arrangements, marble counters and Japanese koto music whispering from the speakers, discourages hysteria.

As she runs water into the sink she hears the door to one of the stalls unlatch, and composes her face as a woman walks towards her. She is in her early thirties, her chin-length blond hair carefully combed and highlighted, wearing a taupe dress with gold buttons down the front and a sleek gold belt. She looks elegant and expensive, and Fiona is surprised when she stumbles in her strappy shoes, then veers away from the row of sinks, neglecting to wash her hands. She stands in front of one of the mirrored panels and begins twisting her shoulders back and forth, attempting to check the zipper on the back of her dress, and rummaging in her tiny reflective evening bag.

"God, what a party," she says to Fiona's reflection in the opposite mirror. Her words come in a rush, blurring together at the ends of the sentences. "You'll excuse me, I've had a few glasses of wine. Just a few. I can't believe this, I look like shit. And these are new shoes—Ferragamo—and they're killing my feet. Why don't they have these parties on weekends anyway? Because I've been wearing my makeup all day and how can they expect me to look good at night too? God, I look a wreck. Meeting all those people, too. And my husband—you know my husband?"

"No," Fiona says, watching her. "You are—?"

"Oh sorry, I thought everyone knew. I'm Cynthia, Jack Warren's wife. His *second* wife. Everyone out there sure knows. Don't you know who he is? My husband, he's president of the Warren Group. You've seen articles in the paper about him, he's a big supporter of the arts. There was a profile in the city magazine last month. He's the man in the wheelchair."

"Oh." Fiona remembers a man in a roomy suit jacket, with shining silver hair swept back from his brow and a strong face, sitting in a wheelchair among a group of people near the centre of the room.

"Yes, that's my husband," the woman continues, tilting her chin at her reflection, unscrewing the cap off a tube of mascara. "*I* was the one who took care of him after his accident, you know that? No one gives me credit for that. We were friends for years, when he was married to that other woman, and she left him after he lost the use of his legs. And people out there dare to talk about me like I took him away from her just because he's got some money and he's famous. Because he's famous, you know, people talk about him. But I was there when she left him. You believe me, don't you?"

177

She swivels around to face Fiona, her lip trembling, her legs apart, and Fiona lifts a finger to a spot under her own eye, tapping it lightly. "You have a bit of mascara—right here."

"Oh," the woman says, starting to giggle. She pulls out a tissue and dabs at her face. "Is it gone now?"

"Yes."

"So just because I'm his second wife, and not his first," the woman continues, in the compulsive manner intoxicated people have of fixating on an idea and assuming it is as interesting to others as it is to them. "They think they can talk about me like that. They're all talking about me out there, you don't believe me? Go ahead and ask. They'll tell you. 'Oh, that Cynthia,' they'll say, 'she's such a little gold-digger', blah blah blah. It's not true though. I've loved him for a long time, even when we were friends. He didn't know it then, but I've always loved him."

"I know," Fiona says. Suddenly she wants to get away. She checks her watch; it is barely eleven-thirty. If she leaves now she can hail a cab outside and be at the airport before midnight and, brave still with wine, she can fly to Raymond's city to tell him that she loves him. Yet she knows in her heart that it is too late. *Men aren't the same as women*, Frank, her colleague at the college, said to her. *Women, you tell them that you love them when they're thinking of leaving you, and there's the distinct possibility that they will then melt and change and come back to you. It doesn't work that way with men, it works opposite.*

She knows she will sober up once she gets into the taxi and do the sensible thing instead. Go home, drink a glass of water, swallow an aspirin, go to bed. That she considered flying to Raymond's city is enough to sustain her. Suddenly she feels quite cheerful again, and inspired with purpose.

"Well, good luck," she says to the woman, picking up her purse from the counter.

"Are you leaving? Nice talking to you," the woman says. She is putting on lipstick rather more successfully than she was applying mascara, and she is busy gazing at herself in the mirror, rubbing her chestnut-coloured lips together.

Fiona hesitates at the door of the reception room, glancing inside to see if Raymond's employee is still there, but she doesn't have time to linger. She collects her coat, walks out into the night where it has begun to rain. A sweet light drizzle falls through the air, and the ski lights on the mountains twinkle. She stops at the curb, holding her hand high for the taxi which, with perfect timing, blinks its headlights and slides obediently towards her, much like a coach in a fairy tale.

10.

I saw your wife in a photograph in a women's magazine delivered door to door. The magazine featured a series of articles on working women, and there was a photo and a short interview with Helen. She talked about the importance of balancing her home life with her career, and the comfort of having a loving, supportive husband. "My marriage remains the most important thing in my life," she was quoted as saying.

The photograph showed her wearing cream-coloured slacks with sharp creases, and a cashmere sweater stitched with pearls. She was sitting at the bottom of a stairwell with her legs crossed at the knee, her chin in one hand. Her mouth was full and slick with lipstick, her cheekbones rounded, the skin around her eyes faintly crumpled like old Kleenexes. She had the loveliest hair I had ever seen, so pale, like the hair of fairy-tale princesses who grew up to marry the men of their dreams.

⌇

I had never been in love until the night I met you. And then everything I had understood up to that night, everything I thought I knew, was suddenly and violently re-ordered. I thought I would remember aspects of that night forever. I remember the unbecoming blue eyeshadow that another woman in the room was wearing, and the man in the tweed jacket who prodded the arm of a man with a nose ring and said, *It's you, you're bad luck, you brought the rain with you*, and the lightning that streaked the windows of the reception room like blood along the blade of a knife. I remember the orange brandy that slipped back and forth in the snifter I was holding, and most of all I remember the shock I received when you shook my hand.

In a way, the fifteen months that followed were the

happiest times of my life. Some afternoons, cleaning the apartment before your arrival, stocking the fridge with your favourite white wine, I realized I had never been happy before. And so I wasn't disturbed at first by my increasing interest in your marriage. Sometimes I would lie awake in bed imagining your hands in your wife's hair, your eyelids trembling under her kisses, your fingers throbbing between her thighs. I imagined Helen's tired face buried in the back of your neck where you smelled most like the colour green, and the positions in which, half-waking in the night, you would coax her limbs. I imagined the times you took her roughly and how she responded as though you were a stranger she had met once and desired; the times you touched her with respect because she was a woman and your wife.

After a while I realized I wanted to watch you with your wife, making love to her. The only thing I wanted more was something I was beginning to understand would never happen—I wanted to watch you giving Helen the worst news of her life; I wanted to hear you tell your wife that after fifteen years of marriage, you would have to leave her because you had met someone whom you loved more.

ભ

My fantasies of your wife grew increasingly intimate and violent. I wanted to strip Helen naked, to familiarize myself with her body, her responses; I wanted to put my face against her chest and listen to her heartbeat climb towards orgasm, and then the slowing of her breath and pulse. I wanted to examine between her thighs with the probing interest of a physician, to explore the inches of her skin for marks, moles, wrinkles, to measure the proportion of muscle to fat, the density and porosity of her skeleton.

I wanted to know Helen's body so well I could climb in and zip up her skin around me. Did your wife blush when she was excited or embarrassed? Did she have cellulite on the backs of her thighs, was she prone to eczema or chapped lips in winter? Was she phobic of storms, crowded spaces, spiders? Like a method actress, I wanted to study her gestures, the series of tics one has without being aware of them. Was she vain about her hair, and did she draw attention to it by frequently tucking it behind her ears;

sweeping it off her brow, tossing it over her shoulder? Did she bite her nails or pick the dry scabs of lipstick off her lower lip with her teeth? I had to know: what was it about her that held your love?

I had one fantasy I could hardly bear to admit even to myself. In this, I would be standing behind a pillar in a parking lot, watching a set of keys being knocked out of Helen's hand as she walked alone to her car after work. It would be a frigid night in winter, the sky outside deep and romantically starred. I imagined myself watching unflinchingly as the white, faintly circled skin of Helen's throat met the mirroring flash of a stranger's knife. He would shove his hand swiftly under her skirt, fumble past the silky layers of lingerie for her hole. He would leave forever an impression of his identity inside her—her vagina would remember forever the whorl of his thumbprint, and the bladed edges of his nails. And then his penis, rough and blunt as a bat. The sounds she would make, twisting in his arms, would sound from where I stood like sex, like the sounds I imagined she sometimes still made with you.

In this fantasy Helen did not really fight back; I

sensed it would spoil the vision if she did, injecting notes of terror and strength that would make the scene seem too real. I only wanted to see the pain in her face, the strange stillness that the worst pain can sometimes produce, the masking of her features. I wanted to see an approximation of what her face might look like in the instant you told her it was over, fifteen years of marriage, over, even while knowing that no violation of her body could produce quite the same depth of pain in her face.

The image of the stranger rubbing his face between Helen's breasts, breathing in her scent of soap, perfume and perspiration; the marks like petals he pressed with his fingers on her skin; the exposure of her vagina in the parking lot, the hair between her legs likely darker than the hair on her head, dishwater blond, soft and furred—this seemed the closest I could come to you, this seemed the only place I could find you where you dwelled.

k

Not long after we first met I had said, *What if one day you leave me. What if one day you disappear, refuse to answer my phone calls, refuse to see me.*

And you had said, *Yes, that will happen.* And then you had laughed into my incredulous silence. *When I'm dead. Then you'd know I was dead.*

I never asked you what you meant, if you meant dead dead, or if you meant when you had become dead to me. Because when you did leave you had not died, at least not in the way I understood death, to be final in preventing your return. It was true there was something preventing you, but it was inside your living self, and you never told me what it was. Some days I thought it was because I had meant nothing to you, that your visits to me had become a routine you found troublesome. Other days I thought it was because you loved me and this love was destroying you, as my love for you was destroying me. I had no proof either way; perhaps it was something else entirely, something that had nothing to do with me.

∽

Your departure brought back a memory. Once, when I was eight years old, I had read my mother's diaries. They were chunky, cloth-bound books with waxy pages covered in her handwriting, and they had been stuffed into a plastic garbage bag and secured in a bottom of my closet. Wedding albums, old clothes and records all found their way in boxes and bags into my closet, which had more available room than the one in my parents' bedroom, and my mother must have thought I would never notice the diaries or, if I did, would not be able to understand their contents. It was true I did not understand much of what I read, but I did know there was a married man who was not my father, someone my mother had loved at one time—it was difficult to figure out when, since none of the entries were dated. Nothing, it seemed, had ever happened between them. Numerous times he asked her out for lunch, for dinner, but she had mostly refused. Once he tried to give her a bracelet and she had, weeping, returned it. Who was the man? I somehow had the impression of a professor, a bespectacled man with straight, sandy hair combed back from his forehead. "I must not, it is not right, I will not let myself," she had written at the end of several diary entries. What had happened? Innocently I asked her, and yet it was not innocence, because I understood in some indefinable but definite way that I now held power over her.

That night, before my father came home from work, my mother sat in front of the fireplace and took a strong pair of scissors—the ones she used to cut fabric—to the diaries. There were dozens of the little books, spilling out of the garbage bag, their pages smelling of tea leaves and rose-scented hand lotion. She cut the pages in halves and quarters, a meticulous job that took over an hour, in silence, to complete. When they were all destroyed she piled them back inside the bag, heaved it into her arms and took it outside to the curb, her slippers slapping down the stairs. I felt the significance of what had happened, although I could not have put it into words. I did understand that my mother had now lost something she could never get back, and that life could not be the same again for her.

♡

In the months that followed the end of the affair, I thought I saw you, or your wife, everywhere. Your face reflected back at me from the faces of men passing me on the vibrant street at lunch hour. Their eyes flashed like mica, their faces were similarly shaped, and I thought for the first time that in many respects you must be absolutely ordinary, otherwise how could so many strangers bear your resemblance? Yet none of them survived a second look. And so it went for your wife as well. One day I thought I recognized Helen at a neighbourhood health food store, standing at the counter and pointing to a tray of muffins. What was she doing in this city? But when the woman swept back her hair her face was merely that of another pretty woman who was beginning to show her age. I wondered, uselessly, what I would do if I ever did meet your wife again—would I be kind or vicious, selfless or sadistic? Would I pretend nothing had happened, or that you had said words and made promises you never had?

Some mornings I stood in front of the mirror in my bathroom, recalling the expression on Helen's face in the photograph. She had been smiling, but still there lingered an expression of gravity around her eyes, the corners tugged downwards—a serious, listening expression, one I imagined a counsellor or a psychologist might wear. Was it intentional, did it reveal something about her personality, or was it merely an accident of the light? I could easily imagine

Helen looking at you in that way at the end of the business day, when you unburdened some of the things that had happened in her absence. I stood in front of the mirror, which bent at the sides so I could see my profile from the left and right as well, flexing the little muscles around my own eyes until I thought I saw your wife looking back at me.

Once I was walking down a main street towards my studio when I glanced up at a billboard and thought I saw you in the advertisement, your back turned to the stream of traffic and passersby below. There was the width of your shoulders I had stroked and kissed, the line of your back, the straightness of your waist. I walked around the block and stood beneath the billboard, next to the makeshift tent a homeless person had built for himself among the bushes at the billboard's base. It wasn't you, of course, but the man in the advertisement held his body in the same way—erect, attentive—and had an almost identical build. The ad was for something abstract: the future of telephone technology. There were several images of the man, both shrunken and blown-up— walking on a beach, stepping up a flight of stairs that ended in mid-air, gliding through a gelatinous bubble in which a flame-coloured fish flicked its fins. I felt a heart-stopping surge of pain and desire, and yet this man had nothing to do with you, as perhaps you yourself no longer had anything to do with my fantasies.

&

It has taken more than a year for the intensity of the obsession to pass. I still think of you daily, and I continue to believe there will never be anyone else for me, but at least when I look in the mirror I see only my own face, and when I look into the faces of men who pass me on the street I usually see strangers who don't resemble anyone else I know. Often I wonder if you ever think about me, or if you have told your wife anything of our relationship, but I accept that these are among the many things that I will never know.

I will never have a chance to know Helen; my intimacy with her has been obscene and one-sided. We lavished our love and our care on the same man and yet, our hands and mouths sliding over your skin, we did not touch each other.

And I will never know what it would be like to be with you, not in the way we were together, but in the way that a wife is with her husband, or a mother is with her family. Would I have some night lain awake beside you, as my own mother had lain beside my father when I was a child wakened by her sobbing, her screaming that she did not love him, that we would be better off without him? Of all the possible futures in front of me, a life with you is one that has been taken away, and I will never know if it would have held the most happiness, or the least.